THE FOURTH LEVEL

FALLEN ANGEL

BOOK SIX

I0619563

NICHOLAS HUNTLEY

This book is a work of fiction. Any reference to historical events, real people, or real places is used fictitiously.

First Edition, August 2018

Copyright © 2020 by Nicholas Huntley

nichhuntley.ca

WHITEWOLF PUBLISHING

The use of any part of this publication reproduced, transmitted in any form or by any means, electronic, mechanical, photocopied, recorded, or otherwise, store in a retrieval system, without prior written consent of the publisher – or in the case of photocopying, a license from the Access Copyright (Canadian Copyright Licensing Agency), One Yonge Street, Suite 1900, Toronto, Ontario M5E 1E5 – is an infringement of the copyright law.

Paperback ISBN 978-1-988765-19-8

Digital ISBN 978-1-988765-22-8

All rights reserved. No part of this book may be reproduced in any form for commercial gain by any electronic or mechanical means, including information storage and retrieval systems, without permission in writing from the author. The only exception is by a reviewer who may quote short excerpts in their reviews.

The text of this book is set in Times New Roman.

"Who among us has never looked up into the heavens on a starlit night, lost in wonder at the vastness of space and the beauty of the stars?"

– John Ellis Bush

Act 1, Scene 1

The sovereign of the Solar System shined brightly with all its might in the pox of pure white helium plasma that composed its surface. Flares danced around where atomic fusion took place, emitting radiation in waves after waves of endless ultraviolet light. The star of our existence sat idle and center in the great void.

To the right of this king was the planet as grey as quicksilver, Mercury, orbiting closest to the Sun and wrinkled in craters against its dull ash grey surface. A jet of ice passed the planet, glistening and extending its tail as it got closer to meeting its face to the Sun. The comet outgassed and demonstrated a light blue aura before burning up and disintegrating into dust.

"I'll tell you what, Barry," Charlemagne remarked, distancing himself from the cosmic view as he withdrew the VR goggles from his eyes, "you might have just set me back into an astrological phase."

Barry laughed at his old friend's remark, holding his arms crossed and watching Charlemagne with his new tool.

"The resolution needs some adjustment, but other than that, it'll make my days watching the skies a little easier," Barry replied.

"It should be more interesting than staring at a computer screen when it comes to visual observation, and it'll make you feel like you're right up there in the heavens."

"Nothing can make me feel like I'm truly up there... in the endless void of space," Barry mesmerized, taking a deep sigh. "At my age, this would be the best and only method to feel like an astronaut."

"Don't say that, Barr," Charlemagne replied. "The same could have been said to Buzz Aldrin and Neil Armstrong before they made it to the moon. The world changes…"

"… not fast enough," Barry remarked, turning to walk over to his workstation. "You know how it is…"

Charlemagne looked over to his friend with both a sense of pity and an equal level of empathy, understanding how it was. Barry sat down at his rolling desk chair and arched over to look at the ground in bitterness.

"We're supposed to be on Mars by now," Barry said, straightening up and leaning back into his chair to look at Charlemagne. "An entire colony, set up and braving the new world out there for us."

"Yes, but those same people also promised us hover cars, but here we are with the latest innovation of *electrical* vehicles," Charlemagne remarked.

"Times were different to push all the power of the United States and Soviet Union combined into a race for the Moon. Now, there's nobody to push anybody. Not that those countries even cracked space travel on their own. There's an equal amount of lack in great people – the world sure as hell could use another Werner von Braun to rub a little intellect into the scientific community."

"The world needs more than just one great person. Anyways, let's not get caught into that. I don't want to depress you – that's not why I come to visit you."

"Yeah, but at least I can vent my frustrations out on the greed of profit-driven men with you up here. We're too lucky to be in the town we live in, Charles. Every night I watch the news and become more disillusioned with what the world has become – Brethren of Islam terrorize X country, politicians and media push acceptance of Y. Not that I have prodigy to leave behind in this world, but perhaps you can feel the concern as a father now – what is the future going to be like for your kids? For Diana and Tristan? The future is bleak, Charles."

Charlemagne didn't reply.

"Human talents are being wasted. There's no meritocracy in the lands that used to be great. There's nothing but greed and selfishness from people that claim altruism and selflessness. I hate it. I constantly question, 'Why am I here in this observatory?' but then I'm reminded about the scum of the Earth and feel a little better to be safe in here."

Charlemagne didn't interrupt Barry, choosing to listen instead and nod his head.

"God, why *am* I here?" Barry remarked, standing up and raising his hands up with frustration. "It's been fifteen years since the accident – since the divorce!"

"You're here because nothing has pushed you to leave," Charlemagne replied. "You might not be happy, but you're not miserable enough to do something about it."

"I haven't talked to her since the divorce and I don't think I'll ever get to anymore. I was so… naïve to think that she'd talk to me again. I should never have guilted you into buying me this observatory."

"Guilted me?" Charlemagne replied, smiling and raising an eyebrow. "You never caused me to feel guilty for your misfortunes. You came to me and I did the act of purchasing this place as a friend – more than that, I never wanted you to be up here, but you insisted. I still don't think that living up here is good for your health…"

"Well, it's not much, but at least I still have my intelligence and sanity accounted for," Barry sighed, resting his arms on the rests of his seat.

Charlemagne and Barry looked at each other seriously before cutting into crude laughter.

"You expect me to believe that when on the second year that you were living here, you dragged myself and the board of directors here for that presentation on that extraterrestrial signal transmitter."

"*You* dragged the board up here, Charles! I told you it was a pet project of mine, but you insisted on showing them all. We were chasing jets from the airfield for about two months."

Charlemagne laughed and replied, "Do you remember when the government agents came to the observatory and took us out for that 'drive' and chat?"

Barry chuckled and said, "I thought it was the men in black for sure. I knew we had gone too far into the deep end. I still remember the agonizing fear thinking that this was it and we were done for."

"Men in black… you must have been a bit botched in the head, you loon, to have thought an underground agency had kidnapped us."

"Well, it wasn't comforting when you and the colonel greeted each other like you were old friends. I felt like we were in university again and the dean had just called us to his office for that little accident with Professor Clark and the confetti rocket."

"Oh, Clark never had a sense of humor. Do you know that she's still teaching over there? Same course and same content – I bet even in the same lecture hall. I learned this when I heard she did a talk in Harlech last month."

"Jeez, I haven't been back to the university since I graduated. Is that old man with the combover beard still teaching in the physics department? We had him for our first-year physics course… what was his name?"

"Old combover Professor Keel?" Charlemagne questioned, crossing his arms and leaning back on the table.

"That's the guy!" Barry remarked, laughing. "What a legend. Tell me he's still teaching."

"I wouldn't know. I haven't been around his building. All in all, I believe I'm still banned…"

"Dean Pratt wasn't joking when she said that she was going to ban you from that hall for life then, I suppose," Barry jibed.

"Anyways," Charlemagne replied, laughing. "We're talking nonsense and you're making my sides hurt with all this laughter."

"Oh, come on. You're getting old, old man," Barry smiled.

"We're hardly any different in age, Barry," Charlemagne replied, raising an eyebrow as he crossed his arms. "You wait until you've crossed the mid-fifties barrier, and then you'll see."

"Haha," Barry laughed, turning around and going back to his computer. "Alright then, I think that's enough out of you from today. Don't you have kids to pick up from school or something? I've got to get back to work. There's lots to do before the meteor shower tonight."

"It's still August – they're on holiday for another week."

"Ah, I wouldn't have known that. I don't go out… or have kids…"

Barry began to type at his keyboard. Charlemagne looked at him and rolled his eyes. He then took a deep sigh and gave a saddened frown at his old friend.

"You haven't met them yet, have you?" Charlemagne asked.

"Nope," he plainly replied before chuckling. "I still can't believe it though… you're a dad!"

Charlemagne gave a light laugh and a warm smile.

"Not quite a father, but very much a guardian," Charlemagne corrected. "It's really not as hard as people make it out to be. I have no idea what kept my father back. Granted, I'm fortunate enough to be taking care of some (slightly) mature adolescents and I managed to skip the most difficult part of parenthood, in my opinion: infancy."

"I thought adolescence was supposed to be the hardest part," Barry remarked, fixing his glasses as he continued to type into his computer.

"I would hope not..." Charlemagne replied, stroking his chin. "A part of me thinks that it's harder on the kids than it is on the actual parents. Although, I have experienced some hardships at their sufferings...."

"It's tough being a teenager," Barry sighed. "They're lucky to have somebody as knowledgeable as you by their side – not so lucky for other features."

"I beg your pardon?" Charlemagne questioned, crossing his arms tightly as he looked at Barry smirking. "I'll go ahead and ignore that show of whit and instead get on with what I originally had in mind. You haven't seen the kids, and I feel as though it would be unfair for you to stay cooped up in the observatory all alone for this meteor shower. Why don't you come down for the evening? We can use my telescope and just enjoy the display instead of making a hassle of work and such."

"Sorry, Charles, but I have to monitor the meteorites. I've been running into some greater interference lately, and I can't afford to be away from my station."

"Set the scanners onto auto for tonight and we'll link you from the manor if there are any problems. If anything goes wrong, you'll be right there as if you haven't left."

"I don't know," Barry replied with absolute hesitation. "I don't want to be away from my equipment either. The recent interferences have been almost impossible to fix and I know there's got to be a good reason for them. Tonight is my night to discover something, Charles. I can't walk away from that."

"The interference is probably just solar interference…" Charlemagne suggested. "The Sun has been more active lately and it's doing all sorts of no good."

"No, it's something else, Charles," Barry replied, turning to him with slight irritation. "It's something else, and I just... have high hopes that it'll be something to make my time spent up here worthwhile."

"If tonight is the night, you'll have better access from the manor than alone here. Please, Barry, I'm pleading you to come down and get out of here for once. Meet the kids – they'll love to hear you talk about your well. Well, Tristan would…"

"What about the other?" Barry questioned.

"Diana… she would probably be more fond of you talking poorly of me. She's… it's hard to talk about Diana sometimes because she is truly different than Tristan, and I have some peace with that, but… anyways, that's not important right now. I love both of them, and I would also love if you would come down to meet them. It would mean something to me."

Barry sighed and then said, "Alright, Charles. I'll meet your kids. I'll need to see about getting as much as I can done before this evening and then I'll go down to the manor. If it means that much to you…"

"It's for the best, Barr," Charlemagne replied. "You don't have to worry about missing out on anything later in the night. I promise."

"If you're not doing anything for the next hour or so, we could speed up getting me out of here if you helped me out? I might actually be able to get ready for this surprise outing and you won't have to drive back to pick me up."

"Of course! I still remember a fair bit of this hardware from when we installed it."

"Alright then, but you have to promise me that I won't regret going down, Charlemagne," Barry strictly said, looking across to his friend.

"You have my promise," Charlemagne swore.

Act 1, Scene 2

Diana stood at her bed, putting a water bottle into her backpack along with her laptop, her wallet, and other various random items she might need for the day to come. Tristan entered her bedroom, noticing Diana's intentions to go out. He popped a smile and walked over to her.

"Hey, where are you going off to?" Tristan questioned.

"I told you – I'm going into town to meet up with Moira. We haven't seen each other all summer and she just got back from the States yesterday."

"Oh, I see…" Tristan replied as Diana put on her backpack. "I guess I'll catch you later then."

"Charles phoned Mavis and she told me that he wants us to be here for dinner. Apparently, he has a very important guest coming over and wants us to meet him."

"That's okay, I didn't have plans with anybody anyways…" Tristan remarked with a bit of bitterness. "Not that I *have* friends anymore…"

"You still have me," Diana replied, raising an eyebrow.

"You don't count," he immediately responded, crossing his arms with a frown.

"Don't be so jealous. I'll be back for the meteor shower. We're doing that later though and I haven't forgotten about it."

"Alright," Tristan said, sighing. "I guess I'll… I don't know. I'll find something to do, just don't worry about me."

"Good," Diana replied, walking past him. "I'll catch you later."

Tristan spun around as he watched Diana leave. He then took another sigh before turning back around and sitting at her bed.

"I love you too," he murmured to himself before laying back.

Diana walked down the hall with excitement, entering the foyer and then quickly managing her way through the ground floor into the kitchen.

"See you soon!" Diana said to Mavis as she passed her.

Mavis jumped out of surprise as she turned around with a tray in her mitten-covered hands. She watched as Diana made her pass by her and went into the closet going down to the garage.

Diana walked into the loft of the garage and slid down a ladder. She then went to one of the two bicycles parked near the exterior garage door. The interior garage door looking into the pen was open and Zephyr was roaming around nearby the outside of the fence.

"I'll catch you later, Zeph," Diana shouted, picking up her bike and setting it down before hopping onto the seat.

Zephyr ignored her and continued to nibble at some grass under the late summer heat. Diana got onto her bike and started to make her way down the driveway before slipping through the open gates. She peddled down the street and made her way onto the bridge. She then made her way past the open suburbs of ranches beneath the plateau that held downtown Allabrese. She peddled uphill and came into town where a gentle wind was picking up along Main Street.

Diana got off her bike and stepped onto the sidewalk with flow. She then started to walk around town square before going over to Cabernet Head Office. Diana spotted a girl with red hair in front of the office building as she started to safely cross the street. She then decided to sneak up on her as she got closer to her without her noticing. Diana raised a smile the closer she got, gently moving with the sound of her bicycle gears turning as she eyed Moira.

Moira's saffron hair was cut short, but her glasses were much the same. The length of her hair went down to her shoulders.

"Hey there!" Diana greeted as she finally turned around.

"Oh my God!" Moira remarked, bringing a hand to her chest as she jumped.

Moira then raised an embarrassed smile as she looked at Diana and walked over to her.

"No horse?" Moira questioned.

"Not the most appropriate mode of the transportation when you're going to go meet up with a friend," Diana replied. "Besides, Zephyr is the jealous type."

"Right," Moira replied, looking back at Diana as she put a hand on her waist. "You're looking a lot different than in June."

Moira looked at Diana who had also shortened her hair and had a bit of a tan. She was dressed in a white tank top underneath her denim jacket with the sleeves rolled up. She also wore khaki shorts and white shoes.

"Thanks," Dian replied with a warm smile, scratching her head as she looked at Moira. "You look older too – definitely taller."

"I might be just as tall as you," she replied with a confident smile.

"I doubt it," Diana quickly replied, lowering her hand and retaining a smile as she looked to the side.

"We'll just have to measure and see some time," Moira replied.

"No, we don't."

"Sounds like you fear the truth," she laughed. "Anyways, I guess there's no point in asking how you are since we haven't exactly been in the dark to each other for too long."

"Yeah, and you know how Egypt was for me (even if you barely believe me), and I know what was up with you."

"I'm sorry I missed your birthday," Moira replied. "Happy belated though. One week late isn't too bad, is it?"

"It wouldn't be the latest some people gave gone," Diana remarked, rolling her eyes. "I'll be sure to wait until late September to say the same."

"Sounds fair," Moira replied as they started to walk together back the way that Diana came.

"So, what's up in general then?" Diana asked.

"A bit of relief to be back in town, really. How about you? You're still as smiley as when I left you. I guess all's good at the great big mansion, right?"

"Everything has been fine at home. I love it there, I really do," she replied. "What about you? How was your life in the little big city?"

"It was nice to see my mom," Moira replied as they crossed the street. "Are we still going to go to the Summer Festival, or is that a no-go for today?"

"It's a no-go," Diana replied. "Charles wants me back before dinnertime to meet a friend of his."

"And afterwards? We could catch the meteor shower later in the night. You must get a better view from the other side of the river, I think."

Diana's stomach churned as she found herself conflicted. She immediately shook her.

"I'm sorry, but I promised Tristan that we would do something later tonight. I kind of left him on his own at the mansion, and he seemed a bit bitter about me abandoning him."

"Aw, poor baby," Moira replied as they stopped across from the entrance to the civic center. "Why didn't you invite him to come with us? He's practically my friend too after the end of last year."

"Please don't remind me about that," Diana requested. "I mean, a part of me does like it when it's just us hanging out as friends, and another loves that Tristan spends time with me- us. I just- I feel bad for him as if I'm to be blame for what's happened to him."

"Don't feel too bad. It's not your fault. It was Peter's and those dumb rumors of his before he graduated. He needs to grow up- to be mature like Tristan instead of spiting him. Tristan is just a protective brother, like mine, and there's nothing wrong with that."

"Yeah, my protective brother…" Diana replied, losing eye contact with Moira as she looked to the side. "So, what do you want to do instead of going to the festival then?"

"I've got a great idea," Moira replied with a smirk. "I'll be honest, when you messaged me this morning saying that you weren't able to stay long, I wasn't that bummed out. I've actually been dying to show something off to someone."

"Oh yeah, and what's that?" Diana questioned.

"Come on, I need a good Wi-Fi connection beforehand. Let's go to the corner café," Moira said, rushing off.

"This better not be internet cats again," she groaned.

Diana parked her bike and secured it before following Moira through the park. Diana remained silent as Moira dragged her to the corner of the Frontier Caravan, a small rural coffee shop with black Georgian windows, light blue wooden paneling in the exterior, and a small group of people sitting around inside and outside, enjoying both ice cream and other treats in the late summer noon.

"Is that Mr. Rochelle?" Diana questioned, squinting across the intersection as she made out one of the high school English teachers from their school.

"You bet it is. Come on, let's hide in this bush."

"I don't understand. Is he your surprise?"

"No, but my surprise did rely on him being at his usual hangout spot," Moira replied, entering the park again as she dropped into the prone position. "Come over before he spots you."

Diana rolled her eyes and walked over. She dropped down and watched as Moira took off her own backpack. She removed her laptop from within – a thick, modern-looking laptop. She then opened it up and typed in her password at a blink of Diana's eye.

"I had so much spare time on my hands while on the road that I just *had* to put it to good use. So, I picked up some books, and, well, you'll see the rest," she replied, opening a console command window on her computer.

Diana formed her suspicions over what this 'surprise' might be as she watched her friend type into her laptop computer keyboard at an incredible pace.

"You're a hacker," Diana remarked as Moira finished.

"You've got that right," she replied. "Take a look at my screen. I've managed to bypass Mr. Rochelle's firewall, and since he didn't have any other protections, I'm setting up a remote connection to his computer, and now... I'm in."

"You're in, as in..."

"I've seized control of his computer via the public internet network. Guess what he's doing right now."

"I don't know... perfecting his manuscript?" Diana guessed.

"Yeah, if you call this four-thousand word, eight-page single-spaced wall of text that he's looking at right now a manuscript," Moira remarked.

"Let me see," Diana replied, getting closer to both Moira and her laptop as he brought between them. "Tisk, tisk, Mr. Rochelle. You lectured us about using a double-spaced twelve-point font format and yet you don't do the same."

"Why don't you write a comment on the side of the document and let him know how you feel?" Moira suggested.

"I can do that?"

"Yeah, I mean, I'm assuming he isn't using some word-processing program from the last century. Go for it!" she replied, checking. "Here we go," she said, clicking. "Let him know how you feel."

Moira moved her hands away from the laptop and allowed Diana to have some fun. With hesitation, Diana moved her hands over the keyboard and began to put together rude words to get her vengeance against her English teacher.

Diana's eyes moved up and over the laptop screen with Moira's as they looked over to where Mr. Rochelle was sitting down inside the café. His face was fresh with terror as if he had just seen a ghost. He started to look around as the two of them burst out laughing.

"Let's show him some criticism," Diana said with a sly smile, looking through the rest of the manuscript as she squeezed the document for everything she could criticize.

Diana looked up in the next minute, pausing and watching for a second as Rochelle brought his laptop from his lap to the table in front of him. He started to look around the café, questioning some of the patrons before pressing around at some of the buttons. Diana and Moira laughed, especially when he tried to unplug his laptop from the nearby socket, thinking it'd do him any good.

"Alright, I think that's enough," Moira said as Mr. Rochelle closed the laptop and started to pack his things. "You're having too much fun with this."

"Isn't that the point?" Diana replied, looking over at Moira.

"I suppose, but he's leaving now. Let's back out before he sees us," she added, closing her laptop and hiding it in her backpack.

Diana and Moira got onto one knee before stepping back and going into the park to avoid being spotted. The two of them laughed lightly as they walked over to the fountain in the center of the park and sat down.

"Imagine what you could do with that sort of power," Diana remarked.

"It's a lot of power, but there's a lot of legal repercussions that come with it. My dad told me about them after I tried to play a practical joke on him this morning. He gave me a stern lecture about all sorts of legal talk."

"How did you get caught?" Diana questioned, looking at her as she took off her glasses to wipe her eyes.

"I was a little sloppy, and besides, as soon as he suspects anything wrong with the internet or his computer, I'm the first he blames since he knows I'm a computer geek."

Diana looked at Moira. Her freckles showed against her white skin. She had a different appearance than with glasses. Diana looked past her and over to a black van parked outside of the only hotel in town, at the opposite corner from the café, between the civic center and library. On the side, it had the logo of a pizza parlor unfamiliar with the town, named 'Papi's Pizza' with various expensive looking machinery sitting atop. Diana frowned at the van.

"What the heck is that?" Diana questioned, nudging Moira with her arm.

"Well, that isn't suspicious at all," Moira replied, observing the truck as two men in black suits left the three-story hotel.

One entered the back of the van while the other seemed to have disappeared behind the right side.

"Since when does Allabrese own a pizza shop?" Diana remarked.

"Since when do pizza deliverers dress in suits?" Moira added, standing up and walking towards the van.

"Whoa, where are you going?" Diana questioned, forcing Moira to stop and turn to her.

"Relax, I'm just going to get a better look," she replied, turning her neck to face Diana before continuing through the park to get over.

Diana rolled her eyes and stood up to go after her. Moira stopped just at the side entrance to the park, standing under the archway and moving towards the archway pole as she observed the van. Diana arrived to her and grabbed her arm, but she got her to let go her.

"We don't need the intimidating G-men to start harassing us," Diana remarked, looking at the truck with fear.

"What's wrong? Scared they're going to spy on you?" Moira taunted, looking at Diana. "Are you scared that they're going to see all of your deepest, darkest secrets?"

Diana looked at her with annoyance. She then looked back to the van. Moira shook her head at him before moving her sights back to the van.

"They're not even moving. They must be listening in on something nearby," Moira described, looking around for possibilities.

"Look, if they're cops, they're probably just doing some investigations into the Medicis," Diana reasoned.

"I'm not surprised if that's the case – this town has a mobster problem," Moira said with a sigh.

Diana's frown deepened at her friend's remark.

"Let's find out if that's true," Moira added, bringing her backpack around and onto the ground.

Moira rummaged through her backpack and took out a small black object.

"Do you see that black box underneath their van with the label that says, 'Do not touch' in bold? I need you to open it and insert this doo-hickey inside."

"No way, you're insane," Diana objected. "What happened to acting within the law?"

"I never said I would do such things – I said that my dad lectured me and I listened. I didn't say that I'd comply. It's not like I'm going to do anything illegal. Now be a good sport and help a sister out."

Diana continued to frown at Moira as she held the small object in her hand. It looked like a USB drive, but the connector was smaller and there was no chip.

"We're going to find out what these cops are doing. Either I go over there and force me to walk back, or you go and we save a bit of time – lessening the chance that we get caught. You wouldn't want me to get caught, would you?"

"I'm thinking about it. I'm not against it, but fine. Give me the stupid chip."

Diana took the small drive into her hands and took a deep sigh as she faced the road. She looked both ways before crossing and made her way to the other sidewalk. She then started to walk down, looking over to Moira on the other end as she sat down at a park bench and got her laptop out. Diana felt increasingly nervous as she got closer to the van. The other cop that was behind the van's right-side had disappeared. Diana thought about passing the truck and going against Moira's wishes, but she weighed the consequences of each option.

Quickly and quietly, Diana stepped down from the sidewalk as she got to the truck and she kneeled down to pretend to tie her shoe. She untied them and then opened the small box underneath the truck. She started to insert the chip into every available socket. Once it finally fit in one, Diana quickly closed the box and tied her shoes. She then stood up and turned around, jumping back and freezing with terror as she noticed the tall figure that was over her. The man had legitimate white skin, a cold stare, and no eyebrows. He looked down at Diana with fierce intimidation, causing Diana to turn around and cross the street instead. A car honked at her, forcing her to jump back before running to the other end. She then tried to regain her cool as she walked over to where Moira was. Diana turned around to see if the figure was still looking at her before she sat down. He wasn't. He had disappeared.

Diana sat down next to Moira and still felt cold from the brief encounter. Moira hadn't even acknowledged that she had returned as she was typing away at her computer. She looked over to Moira's screen with fear. The skin on her arms was fresh with goose bumps and even the summer sun couldn't warm her up again.

"Alright, I'm in. What is Big Brother doing in Allabrese?" Moira questioned herself.

Diana didn't care. She turned her head away and looked around in slight paranoia.

"Oh no!" Moira spontaneously said.

Diana jerked her head over to her.

"What?" Diana questioned.

"They're fighting back against the hack," she said with astonishment, typing furiously. "Oh God, and now they're trying to hack me!"

"Fight back then!" Diana remarked.

"I'm trying, but…"

Moira hadn't finished the rest of her sentence because her screen had turned black. Her hands began to tremble. Moira started to put her laptop into her backpack before looking at Diana and then past her.

"Maybe it's time we leave," Moira said with shock, standing up with Diana as they started to leave.

Diana stood up to join Moira as they started to walk off, but they froze at the sound of a deep voice from behind, telling them to "Freeze."

Moira and Diana turned around and looked over what appeared to be the same white man in a black suit that had frightened Diana earlier.

"Do you have any idea of the amount of trouble you're in," the man warned, stepping forward.

The two of them were frozen with fear as they looked at the strange man. Diana got a better look at him, seeing his deep red lips and sickly white skin. He wore shades that hid his eyes. She had never seen someone so artificial and so tall before in her life. The man walked up to the two of them and instantly grabbed Moira's backpack off of her.

"Hey, give that back!" Moira cried out. "You're in serious breach of my human rights!"

"I'm afraid not. The two of you are under arrest," the man replied, searching her backpack. "Do you understand that it is a federal offence and risk to national security to hack our equipment? Do you understand that?" the man asked, raising his voice.

The man dropped Moira's backpack onto the ground the ground and grabbed her by the arms as she tried to get away.

"Hey, let go of her!" Diana remarked, walking forward to the man.

The G-man flicked his hand at Diana, slapping her in the face and causing her to stumble onto the ground.

"Hey! What the hell was that for?!" Moira shouted at him.

"Be quiet and answer my questions. Tell me, what did you see?! You can get into a lot of trouble for seeing what you saw, now tell me! What did you see?!"

"I didn't see anything. Let go of me! You're hurting my arm!"

Diana put a hand to her cheek before looking back over to the G-man with anger that replaced her fear. However, before Diana could stand up and confront the agent, a single voice caused the agent to stand down.

"Release her," a woman behind the man said in a Londoner accent.

The man frowned, expecting the voice to be of a mere civilian, but he showed the first sign of emotional expression as he looked at the fellow agent behind. She was a she, and she wore deep black shades over her eyes like the male agent. However, she had normal skin like Diana's – perhaps a bit fairer. She also wore a black skirt and stockings instead. She had medium-brown hair tied in a bun.

The man released his grip from Moira's arm as soon as he recognized this woman. Moira staggered back slightly before she could grab her backpack off from the ground.

"We have no business harassing children. Do we? We have work here that needs to be done," the woman said, looking at Diana on the ground before looking back at her (assumed) co-worker.

"Who're you calling kids?" Diana replied.

"Yes, ma'am," the man replied to the woman instead, ignoring Diana as the woman had.

The man turned to the kids and gave them a dirty look. He fixed his suit.

"Consider yourselves lucky. We rarely give warnings… even to children," the man said.

The man then turned around and walked off with the woman. Moira stared at them for a second before looking down at Diana as she lay on the ground still. Diana watched as the pair walked off before bringing a hand to her reddened cheek.

"Are you just going to keep lying there or are you going to get up?" Moira questioned.

Diana turned her gaze to her and frowned.

"I told you it was too risky," Diana replied.

"I'm sorry," Moira confessed, helping Diana up. "Come on, let's just get out of here."

The two started to make their way out of the park. Diana turned around as they got to the end, trying to see if the van was still parked on the curb. It wasn't. The government agents were gone.

Act 1, Scene 3

Diana arrived back at the mansion later in the evening. She parked her bike in the garage and took a deep breath as she looked around and then over to Zephyr. He was lying down inside his pen, looking out to the field as the evening sun came down. Diana took a deep sigh before climbing up the ladder to go to the kitchen storage closet, opening the door and making her way into the house. She then hurried along to go to the dining room.

"Oh, you're back," Tristan said as they ran into each other in the dining room.

"Yeah," Diana replied, taking another sigh.

"You alright?" Tristan questioned, setting down some plates while raising his eyebrows to Diana.

"I'm tired," she simply answered, looking at Tristan.

Tristan was dressed in a burgundy polo with white shorts. His hair was neat and tidied, and a bit of sunlight was shining at him through the dining room window. Diana bit her lips as she looked at him, but turned her head to the archway as Mavis entered the room.

"Thank you, Tristan," she said, walking over to the plates. "Ah, Diana, supper is almost ready. Try and find some nicer clothing to wear as Mr. Cabernet might be a bit upset with you if you're not appropriately dressed for when his guest arrives with him."

"Sure thing," Diana replied, looking down at her grass-stained jeans.

Diana raised her head up and expected to see Tristan in front of her, but he had followed Mavis into the kitchen. She gave a light sigh and then walked out of the dining room to go upstairs.

In the next hour, Diana came downstairs showered and dressed in better clothing. The mansion was quiet despite the chatter of Charlemagne's voice alongside Charlemagne's guest's voice. She listened around for where they were as she came down the stairs to the ground floor of the foyer. Diana came around into the empty living room and then the empty dinette before turning around as she heard voices coming from the back patio.

Diana walked back into the living room and then walked all the way towards the trophy room before the ballroom. She then turned and went outside to join the others. Charlemagne was with Dr. Barry Lambert and Tristan by the pool. Tristan was dressed as he was, but Dr. Lambert was dressed in a collared shirt with the sleeves rolled up as well as tanned trousers. Charlemagne was similar as he always was, but instead of the blazer, underlying vest and bowtie, he simply wore a sweater vest with a tie.

"Ah, here she is," Charlemagne remarked with a pleasant smile. "Barry, I would like you to meet the more mischievous and cunning child in my care, Diana. Diana, this is my old friend, Dr. Barry Lambert."

"Hello, Diana. How're you?" Barry asked, taking Diana's hand and shaking it.

"I'm good," Diana replied in a timid voice, looking over to Tristan who was already sat down at the patio dining table.

The air was cool on the patio at this time of the day. The walls of the mansion helped block the sun from both direction, providing a perfect amount of shade against the humid air. Diana sat down next to Tristan, looking at him before over to the sizzling of the barbecue close to the pool.

The adults were having a discussion about the geography and landscape of the land ahead of the mansion. Tristan looked back at Diana as he slouched back in his chair and they looked more or less (happily) shunned.

"You look good," Tristan quietly remarked, looking ahead of him before looking back over to Diana.

Diana was dressed in a casual white dress with matching flats.

"You don't have to say that every time we have to dress fancy for Charles," Diana replied, feeling her cheeks redden.

"Then stop looking so good," Tristan replied.

Diana rolled her eyes, turning her head away as she started to avoid giving away a smile.

"I'm just saying," Tristan added. "I like to remind you that you always look good."

"Save if for when we're alone, please," Diana replied, feeling her cheeks redden some more.

Tristan gave a light laugh and stopped, looking over to Charlemagne and Barry instead as he zoned out of their conversation entry now and again.

"How was your time with Moira," Tristan asked, remembering as he looked over to Diana again.

"Woof, ask me about it later. The last half was fine, but the first half has a long and unpleasant tale with it."

Mavis stepped outside and went to the barbecue, turning the dial and beginning to serve the main course on a large plate that she then brought over to the dining table. She then left to go to the kitchen, prompting Charlemagne to help her bring the rest of the meal outside.

"Sit with us," Charlemagne insisted to Mavis.

"Oh no, Mr. Cabernet. I would rather not," Mavis replied.

"Mavis, we have this discussion almost every evening," Charlemagne remarked to her with a smile. "Please, remember that you eat with us and not alone. You're a part of this family."

Mavis did not argue with Charlemagne and instead sat down with the rest of them. All five ate and talked well. Charlemagne had started to talk about an old adventure he had with Barry when they were in college as most of the group started to finish their meal. Barry joined in on the conversation after initially being shy and listening, adding to it and correcting details, and then by providing additional commentary as the kids smiled and politely listened.

"I suppose had I not been a Cabernet, I would have been expelled by the dean for damaging his car... or for letting it fall from six-stories," Charlemagne reminisced.

"It was eight," Barry corrected.

"Seven."

"It was eight."

"The moral of the story is, however, to not mess with the personal property of the faculty head... or his coworkers... or the board of governors... even if you think you might be able to impress them," Charlemagne remarked, leaning forward at the table as he held a glass of beer in one hand.

"Unless your surname ends in 'Cabernet,'" Barry added.

"I took the blame for the gang, didn't I?" Charlemagne questioned, letting go of his glass and straightening up in his seat as he crossed his arms.

"I'm pretty sure the only reason we have ever went along with these pranks was because of the natural immunity that came with being around you – you were a sponge for punishment – we always threw the blame at you."

"Well, not every time," Charlemagne replied with reason, raising his hands up. "I can remember quite a few instances when I wasn't there for some of the madder schemes."

The conversation at the table was cut-off by the sound of the doorbell coming from the front door. Charlemagne's ears twitched at the sound and he tried to look through the windows of the foyer to see if he could make out who it was.

"Wow, Charles, did you invite somebody else who's shown up a bit late?" Barry questioned as Mavis stood up.

"Sit down, my dear," Charlemagne replied, standing up on his own. "I can answer the door."

"Nonsense, Mr. Cabernet. You need to let me do my job around here. Please, sit down and keep talking with Dr. Lambert. I will go and answer the door."

Charlemagne looked at her and then sat back down.

"It's most likely just a solicitor anyways – despite the sign," he replied, stroking his moustache.

Mavis left and went over to the door as Charlemagne relaxed.

"Anyways, what time is it?" Charlemagne questioned, looking at his watch. "Goodness, it's only just eight and the sun still shines. Isn't that something?"

"We've still got another couple hours to the meteor shower. Charles and I are planning on watching the shower from his lab. We'll have the telescope to get a closer look – I'll be looking at the big telescope down at the observatory via a remote connection. Of course, you kids are welcome to join us if you'd like. I heard from Charles, Tristan, that you're quite keen for science."

"I'm not much of an astronomer. Besides, Diana and I are going down to the river bank to watch it," Tristan replied with slight shyness as he started to mention Diana.

"Suit yourself. A meteor shower like this is a rare occasion. You might never know when you'll see one again."

Barry finished his last sentence with a dropped down look as he faced ahead of him at who was underneath the trophy room door.

"What is it?" Charlemagne questioned, turning his head at Barry and then over to Mavis as she stood next to another member of the extended family. "Judith."

"Dr. Lambert is here for you, Mr. Cabernet," Mavis remarked.

"Oh, sorry, I didn't realize that I was interrupting something," Dr. Judith Lambert said with slight embarrassment. "I can come back later…" she added, looking at her ex-husband before opening up her purse with a shy smile. "I came to drop-off the data that you wanted me to look at and pick-up the new set you said you had for me."

"Oh, right. Tisk, I thought you were coming in tomorrow. My mistake – let me go and get that for you. It's in my study," Charlemagne said, standing up. "Excuse me, I'll just be a moment. Judith, please make yourself at home."

"Dr. Lambert, can I get you a chair and a drink," Mavis questioned.

"No, thank you," she kindly rejected. "I don't drink and I won't be staying long."

"Very well," Mavis replied, moving over to the table to start clearing some plates.

Diana and Tristan looked over to Barry and then to Judith as they were mostly quiet, avoiding eye contact, and waiting awkwardly for Charlemagne to return. Barry was stunned to see his ex-wife and she was obviously pretending to not look at him. Barry then cleared his throat, which forced her to look at him. She looked at him and then to the ground.

"How are you, Barry?" Judith asked.

"Busy," Barry replied with a nervous expression, "lots of work in the observatory. Not as much as what I had as chief of research. I'm sure you're excruciatingly busy."

"Not as busy as I used to be," Judith replied with a shy smile.

"Here we are," Charlemagne said, providing a hard-drive that he gave to Judith. "Thank you, Judy, for your help. I sincerely appreciate this."

"Not at all, Charles," Judith replied, looking over to him and smiling. "It's a nice break from the meandering of all the other scientists and gives some stimulus."

"Oh, please, if you want a real challenge, try analyzing the current data being pooled through the observatory. Barry can tell you all about it," Charlemagne remarked with a smile before dropping to a frown as he looked at his friend. "Oh, sorry…"

"No apologies, Charles. The past is far behind me," Judith replied. "Thank you again for this data. Remember to analyze mine and let me know what you think. I should heading home now."

"Have you eaten or cooked? Can I offer you some of the delicious food that Mavis has cooked for us? There's plenty to go around."

"Oh, I would love to, Charles. Thank you. It'll save me some time cooking just for myself."

"Let me help you then," Charlemagne replied, taking a side-step before stopping.

"No, allow me, Charles. I'll talk to Mavis on my way out. Again, thank you for this. Goodbye, kids. Barry," she added, nodding to him. "It was good seeing all of you."

"Bye," Barry replied, giving a small wave as she wandered away.

Charlemagne felt heavily embarrassed as he watched Judith leave. He then looked over to Barry who was biting his thumb and thinking to himself.

"I'm truly sorry about that, Barry. I had no idea she was coming over when I invited you. Any legal issues with the restraining order are on me," Charlemagne confessed.

"No, don't worry about it, Charles," Barry replied with a flat face, looking down at the table before over to his friend. "It was nice to see her after all this time. It was like a breath of fresh air. I have no regrets."

Act 1, Scene 4

"Remember, you have a curfew," Charlemagne remarked to the kids as he saw them about to leave from the front door. "Don't be late and don't go too far."

"Don't worry so much. We're just going down to the beachhead in front of the house. We won't be less than two hundred meters away from you," Tristan assured him, holding a backpack around his back as he opened the door for Diana.

"Very well," Charlemagne replied. "Enjoy the meteor shower."

Charlemagne went upstairs while Diana walked out of the house, feeling a bit of the early night cold come over her. Tristan shut the door behind him, letting him walk down the steps with Diana before crossing the driveway and going down the additional steps to the pedestrian gate out of the manor. Tristan opened the gate and let Diana through while he turned around and looked over to the window of the lab. The house was going to shut down its power any second now for the meteor shower, but that wasn't Tristan's concern. He grabbed Diana's hand as soon as he was sure nobody was watching them.

"You don't have to hold my hand," Diana said, feeling her face flush instantly as they stood at the curb of the rough road in front of the mansion.

"But I want to," Tristan replied.

"Sorry, all of this romance coming from you all of the sudden is weird," Diana replied as they started to walk across the road. "Not to mention the fact that this is low-key our first 'date' ever."

"What do you mean?" Tristan replied, smiling at her as she looked at him.

"I'm not complaining," Diana simply replied, giving a warm smile back at him as they got to the other side of the street. "I'm just auspicious of all this sudden romance."

"Who else am I supposed to be romantic with?" Tristan questioned as they started to walk down the wooden steps to the small beach below the cliffs.

"No one," Diana quickly replied for him.

"Exactly."

Diana smiled and stayed quiet as they walked over to find a perfect spot to lay down their towel and sit down.

"So, tell me, what happened between you and Moira today?" Tristan asked as she raised his knees up while Diana stretched her legs.

"Ugh, some weird crap, man," Diana replied.

Diana told him about Moira's new passion for hacking and then told him about the strange men and the black van. She tried to be brief and concise, avoiding any outrageous details that might not make her story believable as she told it.

"I don't believe you," Tristan said with an awkward smile.

"Well, that's your problem and not mine. It was creepy and unsettling, and I'd rather not look at that man ever again. I know he's going to come back in a dream or something, and I'm not going to look forward to it."

"It really happened then," Tristan replied.

"Of course it did. You can ask Moira about it tomorrow too – it was weird."

"Jeez, I guess the organized crime problem really is that bad if that's the case."

"I suppose. Let's just... not talk about it, okay? Although, on the subject, please remind me or tell Charles to jack up the security on the house servers for the next time Moira comes over. She's going to try and hack into the stuff – she's too nosy to resist doing so. If she were to hack into my computer, she's going to find out about us being… you know."

"Being what?" Tristan asked.

"You tell me," Diana replied.

"Best friends?"

"If waking up in bed with you is what you describe as being 'best friends…' Diana sarcastically replied.

"With benefits…" Tristan added.

Diana frowned at him and said in a sarcastic tone, "Yeah, that's what we are… friends with benefits."

Tristan laughed at her and she kept a plain face. He then looked to the town on the plateau with its lights.

"Are you going to look forward to school starting?" Diana asked as she lay down.

"Not really…" Tristan replied, "but I'm bracing myself for it."

"You didn't have to go against your friends for me."

"I was defending you, but it was also not your fault, Diana," Tristan replied. "I did it for me as well. I… I was defending myself – isn't that what you taught me to do – back in Russia when that tourist harassed us at the ski slopes? It doesn't matter. If I had to choose between you and Peter, I would choose you again and again. You've been good to me, maybe even more than I've been good for you."

"Tristan…" Diana replied with a warm smile. "I know for sure that you still wish you could go and hang out with Peter and Aaron instead of me and Moira."

"Yeah…" Tristan nodded. "No offence. Then again, Peter's gone to university, which leaves Aaron almost alone. Maybe I can approach him instead."

"That would be nice," Diana replied.

Diana smiled at him.

"We should go on dates more often," she said.

"Why?"

"Maybe it's just the sudden burst of romance you're hauling around, but I like this level of intimacy where it's just you and me talking."

"You and me talking is all we ever do."

"Then maybe it's because we haven't done this all day that it feels different," Diana confessed.

"You make it sound like you want us to spend less time together," Tristan replied.

"It would make the time we do spend together more special," Diana replied, getting closer to Tristan.

Tristan stretched his legs out and laid back. Diana put an arm around atop of his chest and kept close to him. The couple then stared into the starry night. They lay there, chatting to each other in their streams of consciousness until the lights of the town shut off within an hour.

The natural surrounding was darker and the sky more vibrant with stars pouring across the entire horizon just as it was in Egypt.

In a minute, hundreds of meteors began to cross the barriers of the atmosphere, turning into smoldering rocks with ashes before they joined the outer reaches of the Earth as a forgotten dust. Each one made their pass like fast tears across the face of the galaxy, falling down like stars in the sky until it was all over. Halfway through, Diana and Tristan had begun to kiss on the beach.

The two stopped just before it ended, parting lips and staying close to each other for warmth as they watched the last of the meteors submit to their end.

"Oh crap," Tristan said, closing his eyes with regret. "I forgot to make a wish."

"Aw, poor baby," Diana replied as Tristan opened his eyes.

"I had this planned for the last week though. We'd pick one of the falling stars and make a wish. I even had the wish all sorted out too."

"Relax, it's just a superstition anyways. I doubt whatever you were going to wish for would be the product of fortune."

Tristan rolled his eyes before noticing a bright ball ahead and high up in the sky. It was small, smaller than the sun or even the moon, but slightly bigger than any stars above them.

"Look, there's another one," Diana said, pointing up to the bright and large shooting start as it trailed forward. "Make your stupid wish."

Tristan looked at Diana with a small glare and then back up to the rock as it flashed over town.

"I wish... to be with Diana Anne Cambridge forever," Tristan said, looking back to Diana with the same glare. "Not so stupid of a wish now, is it?"

The rock continued to flash, getting brighter as it created a medium blue glow in the sky like lightning that persisted.

"Uh... it's still falling," Diana remarked, ignoring Tristan for a moment.

The two simply watched in the next seconds as the flashing bright rock passed over them, leaving behind a trail of smoke over the water and beach before all the light died out and it was over, or so they thought.

The couple looked at each other before jumping at the sound of an explosion coming from behind them with a gust of wind that slid above, causing the bushes atop the cliffs to give a sharp split-second rustle.

"What was that?" Diana questioned.

"I think it was a landing," Tristan replied, leaning forward to stand up as he took Diana's hand. "Come on, let's go make sure it didn't hit the mansion."

Act 2, Scene 1

"I'm sincerely sorry about what happened earlier in the evening," Charlemagne confessed to his friend, picking up his eye from the eyepiece of his advanced hobby telescope.

"What do you mean?" Barry replied from the stool at Charlemagne's computer.

Charlemagne was outside on the balcony of the makeshift lab, while Barry was inside next to the doorway on the computer.

"I'm talking about Judith. I completely forgot that I had asked her to come over later today when I invited you. It was not my intention to have you two see each other."

"Ah, don't worry about it, Charles. I don't care. I like seeing her… it got me thinking…"

"About what?" Charlemagne questioned.

"Maybe it's time that I retire from the observatory. Maybe it's time that I go out and pull a Charlemagne – see more of the world, try something new – that kind of thing. I've spent the last fifteen years of my life locked up in that place, and I don't think I want that anymore."

"Are you quitting on me then?"

"No, definitely not. I'm not going to make an impulsive decision – that as much I can restrain myself from being like you," Barry remarked with a smirk.

"Well, I'd support your decision to stretch your legs," Charlemagne replied, ignoring his remark. "You might be good at astronomy, but you're wasting your talents on just one thing. You complained to me about the progress of science in the last decades, and yet you yourself refused to share your brilliance with the world for the last decade and a half or so because of a woman. It's time to act on what you preach, Barry."

"I'm going to see where I can fit in, but nothing is solid yet, Charles. I also think it's fair to let you know and warn you in case I do decide – so it's not a huge shock."

"Why?"

"Well, because you're my best friend, Charles. That's all there is to it."

Barry typed into the computer as Charlemagne silently nodded before looking up to the sky. Every single light on the Cabernet property was shut down in solidarity with the town to allow a clear display of the Milky Way above. Charlemagne squinted into the sky as he noticed a particular bright object – bright like a planet in the sky – but at an odd bluish hue.

"Is the ISS in orbit over us right now?" Charlemagne questioned, looking over to his friend as he began to move his telescope to track the anomaly. "We could have a little fun with them – maybe send them a dubious message or two while we wait for the show."

"I don't think they're over us tonight," Barry replied, standing up from his stool to go outside, "besides, as much as I would love to prank them, the showers are starting right about… now."

The two of them looked up into the sky littered with hundreds of bright dots, seeing dashes of silent meteors cross the barrier of the atmosphere in mere milliseconds. Some went from one side of the horizon to the other, while others barely stretched a portion of that distance. The moment did not last long, but did climax with a display of a dozen pieces of debris at once point until the starry sky went quiet again.

Charlemagne thought to himself carefully as he looked at the sky and scratched his moustache before Barry straightened up from resting his arms on the railing of the balcony.

"Look ahead," Barry said, pointing at a bright disc over town.

Charlemagne's eyes fixated to where Barry pointed, causing him to bend forward and place his arms on the stone railing as he squinted at the flashing orb. The two watched, fully knowing what was going to come next. The light zoomed past above them, sending the night sky into its natural darkness in the next second.

"I better check where that landed," Barry said, moving back into the lab.

"Wait," Charlemagne remarked, but it was too late.

The loud burst in the background caught them both by surprise and caused the mansion to shake in its foundations. The windows vibrated, but the blast was mild and didn't cause any glass to break.

"Nevermind," Charlemagne sighed, moving inside to look at the computer monitor. "I was just going to mention the shockwave."

"It didn't look too big," Barry said, "but it landed."

"Hurry, try and pinpoint its location," Charlemagne replied.

"I'm trying, but the connection on this hunk of junk is abysmal."

Charlemagne rolled his eyes and grabbed his coat from behind the lab door before going over to stand behind Barry at his computer. The monitor showed a satellite map of the country and was loading a point of impact as it traced the trajectory based on the trail left behind.

"Got it!" Barry shouted.

Charlemagne squinted at the screen as it zoomed into a bit of land behind the mansion.

"That's part of the property – let's go claim this rock!" Charlemagne said, slapping Barry's shoulder.

"Hold on," Barry replied, unplugging a tablet device from the computer. "Alright, let's get out there."

Barry took his jacket from the table in the middle of the room, and the two of them left the laboratory to go downstairs. They rushed through the darkness of the mansion to get to the freight elevator going to the garage. Charlemagne went to the key cabinet next to the garage doors to grab the keys to the pickup truck while Barry opened the shutter doors.

"Get the car started, I'll open the gate to the pen," Charlemagne said, tossing Barry the keys as he rushed outside.

Charlemagne went to the gate and opened it before stepping as Barry drove up to him. Charlemagne opened the door and allowed Barry to slide over for him to take the wheel. He then drove after the rock locate somewhere behind the mansion.

Barry focused on his tablet as Charlemagne simply drove straight, waiting for a signal to change direction from his co-pilot.

Charlemagne simply rolled through the rough and dried plains.

"Gah, damn this machine," Barry shouted. "We're going to miss out on this because of this stupid thing."

"Don't mind it," Charlemagne replied. "I think I can see it in the distance."

Charlemagne had started to notice a red-hot glow and started to drive towards it. A large plumage of smoke was towering from what appeared almost like a bonfire in the dark distance.

"I don't understand," Barry said, smacking the side of his tablet in anger. "Why am I getting so much interference?"

"It might just be the airfield," Charlemagne replied as they got closer. "I doubt it's anything."

The truck drove forward as they approached the large crater that surrounded the prize rock. A streak of displaced-earth trailed behind where the rock appeared to have made its impact, and there were small bits of fire and ember surrounding the entire area. The soil was dark, but a warm glow came from it and all the energy that was pouring around. Barry put away his device to the side as he noticed the rock in the middle of the crater. Charlemagne drove as close as he could to the crash site without getting near the flames. He then shut off the engine of the truck but left the lights on and pointing forward to the crater.

The duo left the vehicle and felt the warm radiation of energy against their skin. Charlemagne took a step back and went to the trunk of the car where loads of random bits of equipment had been stored. He picked up a fire extinguisher and began to blow out some of the bits of the fire.

Charlemagne paused as he got closer to the edge of the hole in the ground, looking at the great large chunk of meteor that lay in the center. Barry stepped over to get a better look with him. It was a strange oval shape to say the least and was burrowed into the ground at one end with the other sticking out. Its surface was smooth and slick, and it had a shiny dark silver appearance. However, this wasn't the reason the two of them were so caught up with staring at the extraterrestrial object.

A pulsating green glow was emitting from the rock, demonstrating what appeared to be almost like veins coursing through an apical layer. Barry took up his device to shine it at the rock, reading the results of the temperature to be in the hundreds.

"I should… keep extinguishing the fire…" Charlemagne said as he continued to use the fire extinguisher around the crater.

"I saw some chains in the back of the truck. I'll go rig something up so we can pull it out," Barry replied.

The two split up and Barry walked back to the truck. He put his device into the car and then looked over towards the house as he noticed Diana and Tristan arriving by horseback with Tristan driving and Diana behind him.

"Take it easy, Diana quietly said to Zephyr as he panicked at the fire.

"What's wrong?" Tristan questioned with confusion

"Zephyr doesn't like fire," Diana simply said. "Let's get off here."

Tristan hopped off with Diana, and Diana swung a lead around Zephyr's neck and then dropped the rope.

"Stay here for me, okay?" she quietly asked him before leaving.

Zephyr huffed at her before looking away from the crash site. Diana went over to Tristan as he made his way through the smoldered soil to Charlemagne who had finished extinguishing the last bits of fire around the edges of the crater. A warm glow permeated from the central fire and Charlemagne's face had an orange glow as he glanced up to look over to the kids.

"Ah, I'm glad you've come," Charlemagne said. "We're on land that I own, and that means that this astronomical jewel is ours to keep. I could use your help digging it out, however. Follow me."

"What are you going to do with the rock?" Tristan asked. "I suppose you won't sell it. I mean, you're already rich."

"Oh, heavens no. I'm going to keep it. Something like this is priceless – it deserves to be researched and then displayed to others," Charlemagne replied as he led them back to the pickup truck.

"Definitely researched," Barry replied. "Did you see that glow? Something is definitely going on with this asteroid."

"Glow? Is it radioactive?" Diana questioned.

Barry and Charlemagne looked at each other. Neither of them knew or had thought about the possibility.

"Well, a glow wouldn't mean that it's radioactive…" Barry finally replied after a hesitant pause.

"Why don't you go scan it before we get any closer then," Charlemagne suggested. "I'll get the kids to help out with scooping it out from the ground."

"Sure thing. Here though," Barry said, showing him some chains on the back of the truck. "We can use these to pull it out and lure it into a nest to bring it out of the crater. I'll check for any harmful levels of radiation and see if I can cool it down while you get the truck ready."

"How much do you think it weighs?" Tristan asked as Barry left with a fire extinguisher.

"Oh, probably at most a ton," Charlemagne replied, picking up some heavy-duty chains. "Help me carry this to the front of the truck."

Tristan and Diana helped Charlemagne pick up the chains, and the three of them walked around to the front of the pickup truck where the bright lights of the car shined at them. Charlemagne started to attach the ends of the chain rigs to the front before getting the kids to help him down into the crater to lay each strand out. Each strand was connected to another and each of these were brought around the rock at different angles to nest it in the bundles of iron.

"Nothing on my Geiger counter," Barry reported. "It's still hot though."

The rock was pulsating green and the entire crater was extremely humid. Diana watched as the two scientists talked to each other, looking around the pit and noticing small shards of the meteorite around. She went over to a large piece that stuck out from the side of the crater and looked at it, bringing her fingers close to it to pick it up.

"Unless you want to burn your hands off, I wouldn't touch that," Tristan warned.

"I wasn't going to grab it," Diana replied. "I was just going to see if it was hot or not."

"Well, it probably is. It's probably so hot that it would have melted the skin on the fingers faster than your reflexes could have had you let go."

Diana frowned at him with disbelief. Most of the fire had been put out by now, and the energy in the soil had dissipated to make it harder to see anything, including each other's faces.

"Come on, children," Charlemagne said as he started to walk back up to the ground level. "You won't want to be in the way as the car drives."

Diana and Tristan followed the adults up and out of the way. Charlemagne went into the truck as he left the kids with Barry on the side to watch. The engine of the pickup truck started and Charlemagne started to reverse backwards, coming to a brief halt as the object in the ground objected to being displaced. The chains tightened with the lines at the edge of the crater digging into the burnt soil as the truck stalled for a brief moment before budging backwards as the rock finally gave way.

Charlemagne drove backwards as far as it took for the rock to come out of the pit. He then drove backwards, changing gears to go forward and reverse the truck behind the rock. Once he was satisfied with the position, Charlemagne turned off the car and got out. The kids then went over to him while Barry went to the rock.

"I'm going to need you kids to muster up some strength," Charlemagne requested as he unlatched the chains at the front of the truck. "Especially you, Tristan, for all the time you've wasted in that gym of yours. Each of you are going to take one end of the chains and help drag the rock into the cargo. Do you think you can do that?"

"Yeah," Tristan replied, taking his half from Charles.

"No," Diana responded.

"Give it a shot," Charlemagne encouraged her, "if not, I'll take over."

Diana took her half and looked over to Charlemagne for further instructions as he stood up and led them to the back of the pickup truck. Tristan pulled at his chains, causing the meteorite to nudge and wobble around.

"It doesn't seem that heavy," Tristan remarked. "I mean, I'm sure it weighs a lot, but I think we can do this."

"Good confidence, Tristan," Charlemagne replied, calculating which side each of them would need to take as looked at the meshwork of chains around the rock. "Go back via the rear of the truck and wait for my signal. Diana, go around the left and as far as you can before the chains straighten out."

"Sure thing," Tristan replied as the two split up.

Each of them walked along the side of the truck, fanning out at the opposite direction until they couldn't go any further.

"Ready?" Charlemagne questioned to them.

"Ready!" Tristan shouted back after looking to Diana.

"Pull!"

The kids pulled as hard as they could, each equal halves of weight and feeling some movement be made before a pause was met.

"Keep pulling!" Charlemagne shouted.

A loud thud signaled them that the rock was aboard the truck.

"Stop!" he shouted next.

The kids stopped, letting go of their chains and then took a moment to rest as they both panted lightly. Diana picked up her chains after Tristan, and they both made their way back the way they came. The rock was successfully inside the car. Charlemagne got the kids to deposit their ends into the truck before he closed the back and looked around.

Barry had wandered off around the crater, examining individual pieces of rock that were stuck in the ground. He picked some up with his bare hands, lightly measuring their weight with his palm as he bounced it around. Charlemagne went over to him as he stood up.

"It's light… really light," Barry said. "I didn't expect it to be so light."

"Me too. I had my doubts over whether the kids could pull that rock or not, but they're either stronger than I expected or the rock is indeed lighter than I expected."

"What if it's hollow?" Barry asked, looking around before focusing on the horizon.

"We could drill inside and find its internal composition. A small hole will be all it takes," Charlemagne replied.

"Look over there," Barry said, noticing a type of helicopter in the sky. "We've got company."

A strange vehicle in the air with searchlights flooded downwards was making its way towards them in the field. The two of them watched the craft carefully, seeing if it was going to pass them, go around, or anything else.

"Probably prospectors interested in the rock," Barry remarked.

"Except, since when do prospectors drive advanced helicopters like that?" Charlemagne grimaced, noticing the helicopter to closely resemble a vertical take-off and landing aircraft (V-TOL) instead.

Charlemagne looked at the craft for another second before turning over to the kids talking to each other and noticing the truck lights were still on.

"Oy!" Charlemagne shouted at them. "Shut the lights off of the truck!"

Tristan looked over to him, looking at the lights for a second before going over and into the cabin to fiddle around with a lever inside. The lights finally shut off, letting Tristan slide out of the car and rejoin Diana who had followed him. The two went back to the rear of the truck, and before Tristan could question Charlemagne, he noticed what they were looking at in the distance.

A type of hovercraft was searching around the field near them with a floodlight aimed down at the ground from the belly of the vehicle. The rotors at the side of the machine caused a warm wind to pour downwards underneath it, rustling the tall grass below. The aircraft came close to the crash site, causing Charlemagne to feel anxious until it went away and left them alone.

"I think we should leave," Barry said, putting the rock in his pocket.

"Me too," Charlemagne replied. "We better split up as well."

The two of them went back to the kids to regroup. Charlemagne looked into the back of the truck to notice that a fire extinguisher was still missing.

"Diana, can you go get the fire extinguisher? We need to leave," Charlemagne said.

"What was that?" Tristan asked as Diana nodded and left.

"I'm not sure, but I don't want to be around when they come expecting to plunder a valuable meteorite from my property."

Diana left with this answer and slid down to the bottom of the crater. She picked up the fire extinguisher and started to make her way back up when she noticed the piece of meteor she was going to pick up earlier. The rock wasn't any bigger than her hand. Diana licked the top face of two of her fingers and then pinched the top of the rock. No sizzle.

It was cold. Diana quickly picked it up and put the chunk into her pocket before climbing out of the crater. She regrouped with Tristan and Barry.

"Here you go," Diana said to Charlemagne, handing him the fire extinguisher.

"Thank you," Charlemagne replied, putting it inside. "Alright, let's split up and regroup at the mansion. We'll meet in the garage. Lock the gates of the pen after you come in and be careful."

"Sure thing," Tristan affirmed.

Charlemagne nodded to them and then he and Barry split up and went into the truck on opposite sides. The kids then stepped back as the engine of the truck started and they both watched as they drove off without them or the front lights on.

"Come on, let's go home. I'm tired and we've got to get up early tomorrow," Tristan said, going over to Zephyr.

"Alright then," Diana replied, joining him.

Act 2, Scene 2

Diana and Tristan rode Zephyr across the plains behind the mansion, jumping over the railing of the pen before pausing so that Tristan could hop off and close the gates where Charlemagne had driven the pickup truck through. Diana took over and rode Zephyr back into the garage where Barry was alone with the meteorite in the back of the truck.

Zephyr went past the meteor and was led down the aisle to his stall. Diana then got off and let him rest. She closed the gate after letting herself out, and then she went to a small minifridge at the far corner of the garage to take out some raw carrots.

"See you tomorrow, Zeph," Diana said, giving her horse a snack and petting him on the nose. "Love you."

Diana stepped back over to the rear of the truck, looking over to Tristan as he closed the shutters into the garage and then joined her. Barry looked over to the freight elevators as it arrived with Charlemagne and a small flatbed cart to bring the meteor upstairs.

"My scanners are still picking up interference, Charles," Barry reported. "I don't think it was the airfield like you suggested."

"Curious," Charlemagne simply replied, picking up the chains of the rock to pull it out of the trunk.

Tristan quickly went over to help him, followed by Diana as all three pulled it out to drop onto the cart, causing it to jump up on one side. The green veins of the rock were still noticeable even in the light of the garage, but harder to see.

"I think that'll be enough, children. Thank you for your help," Charlemagne said as he began to remove the chains from the rock.

"No problem," Tristan replied. "We're going to bed. See you tomorrow."

"Goodnight," Charlemagne replied, seeing them off.

"Goodnight," Tristan responded.

Barry looked over to Charlemagne once the kids had left. He then began to laugh.

"I still can't believe you're in charge of two kids," Barry remarked. "God, it's still very funny."

"Oh, be quiet," Charlemagne replied. "Come on, let's get this out of here."

"Uh, how's your hand doing?" Barry asked, noticing Charlemagne holding the palm of his hand on the surface of the metal.

"What do you mean?" Charlemagne replied, retracting his hand.

"Your hand... it didn't burn..."

"It's cooled off... the rock, I mean," Charlemagne said.

"My thermometer said otherwise when I checked a minute ago..."

"Curious..." Charlemagne said with a grim face as he stood up.

Charlemagne and Barry brought the trolley into the freight elevator. They then went upstairs to the ground floor of the mansion. From there, they rolled the cart through the kitchen, towards the foyer, and then with immense difficulty, upstairs to Charlemagne's lab.

Each of them put on latex gloves before trying to pick up the rock, but it was too heavy for the two of them to lift together. Instead, they simply moved the table in the middle of the room to the side to make more room.

Barry gave the rock another scan with his machine, while Charlemagne picked up a laser thermometer of his own to scan the rock. His initial reading gave a similar result to what Barry had been receiving: almost fifty degrees Celsius at the moment.

"There's a lot of energy in this rock… it could be giving us a false reading…" Charlemagne suggested.

"Or, there could be something hotter in the core," Barry pointed out, "like the Earth. Perhaps, there are layers to this rock and there's something hotter inside."

"All the more reason to get a cut into the rock… whatever material this is."

"Don't have any guesses?"

"Well, I'm going to be honest… my first guess had me thinking of a similar light metal that I recall from my trip to Egypt in the summer," Charlemagne said.

"Do you have any samples of this metal?"

"No," Charlemagne replied, "and to be fair, it's not really a metal, but an extremely tough and lightweight alloy. I can't examine this rock on my own to create a full report on its qualities and composition. I believe I'm going to have to involve Judith into this and have the meteorite brought to Cabernet Laboratories."

"I agree," Barry replied. "I can't do much from here either, but I'll try and look over the flight data to see if I can track this rock's history. I'll talk to some of my astronomers in the morning and see if they have any ideas as well."

Barry took out from his pocket a piece of meteor that he had kept.

"I didn't have much room in my pockets, so all I could take with me was this," Barry said, handing it to Charlemagne. "It's a small shard, so maybe you can do some research with this to just research the alloy itself in the meantime."

"Thank you," Charlemagne replied, taking the piece of meteorite and looking at it. "Yes, this is quite similar to what I had laid my hands on inside the Great Pyramid. I've wanted to do more research on this alloy ever since then."

"And now you can," Barry remarked.

Act 2, Scene 3

Diana woke up the next morning to an empty bed. She opened her eyes wide as she examined the empty space next to her, causing her to lean up from her side and look around the room. Tristan was in the bathroom, combing his hair before noticing that Diana had awakened.

"Why didn't you wake me?" Diana remarked, sitting up like a child in her bed.

Tristan shrugged before turning around and saying, "I got up early and didn't want to disturb you."

Diana looked back at Tristan and nodded silently.

"I'm going to go make something to eat. I'll make you something too. I don't think Charles is awake yet, but I heard Mavis in the garden," Tristan said.

"I'd appreciate that," Diana replied. "I'll… get ready for the day then."

Tristan left the bathroom and went through Diana's room to get into the corridor. It was only eight o'clock according to Tristan's phone, which he left behind in Diana's room.

Diana's bedroom felt warm and the sun was bright. Her room hadn't changed much from earlier in the summer, except for the picture on the shelf of Diana, Tristan, Charlemagne, and the old Cabernet exploration crew in Alexandria. On Diana's desk was still a Holy Bible with a bookmark about halfway through.

Diana gave a sigh before getting out of bed to get dressed. She then went downstairs to join Tristan before coming back upstairs with him.

The two then left the mansion at about a quarter to nine, arriving at Lord Phoenix Secondary School via their bicycles in about twenty minutes. The grounds of the school were quiet, which carried a liberating sensation with so much space to themselves.

Tristan and Diana parked their bikes close to the school entrance and then made their way into the main hall. The two walked down the hundred meters to the end, turned left to go towards the cafeteria where a large group of students, mostly seniors from the grade above, but also their own graduating class of thirteen students, including themselves.

The couple entered the cafeteria where chatter between peers was loud, and a division clear amongst the masses of seniors sat away from the sophomores, and people like Moira away from people like Vivian and other popular kids. The graduating class above them was much larger with about twenty-five children, a majority of which were unknown to Tristan and Diana. Their class was large enough to elect a sizeable student council of eight members, all of whom were present.

"This is stupid," Diana remarked as they entered the room. "I have no intention of running for any position on the council, or even voting for that matter. It's a scam."

The pair made their way over to Moira, sitting down next to her with Diana in the middle.

"Have we missed much?" Diana questioned.

"No, you're right on time," Moira replied, looking over to Tristan who looked begrudgingly over to his former clique with a serious look. "Hey, Tristan."

Tristan's ear twitched and he turned his head to the opposite direction to face Moira.

"What's up?" he replied, looking at her with a plain and tired look.

"How was your summer?"

"It was… interesting," he replied. "I enjoyed it. How about yours?"

"Dull," she simply replied.

The screech of a microphone got them and rest of the class to pay attention to where Mrs. Phillips stood with two other teachers and the two student presidents, a boy with light, almost white, blonde hair, and a girl with extremely black hair.

"Good morning, everyone," Mrs. Phillips greeted. "Let's get started. First, I would like to thank our petit Class of 2020 for attending as it is a tradition that some students from the class that will be succeeding our seniors to join them in planning the 'Welcome Back to School' event, especially those wishing to run for student council in the following spring. However, due to the small size of your grade, I've had to make it mandatory that all of you attend, which could be for the better."

Tristan paid close attention, staring at the front as she continued to speak. The microphone was then handed off to the student council presidents. They delivered instructions, requiring all of them to break into groups of five for the four tasks that needed to be done so they could all leave by noon. Moira and Diana quietly chatted between themselves, talking about what happened last night before they were cut off as people stood up to join their groups.

"Diana and Moira," Mrs. Phillips said, causing them to turn to her. "Why don't you join Maia's group and help them unpack the new school agendas and locks?"

"Sure thing," Moira instantly replied, standing up as she eyed Maia with two other girls, including Vivian. "Come on."

"Tristan, we could use your strength to move furniture in the classrooms," Mrs. Phillips added as he tried to join Diana and Moira. "Why don't you go and join Gus?"

Tristan looked over to Diana and Moira. Diana looked at him and showed a frown before leaving with Moira. Tristan looked backed over to Mrs. Phillip and nodded, moving himself over to

Constantine (Gus) Rowan, Aaron Phillips, and three others. Diana sat down at a different lunch table with Moira where several cardboard boxes were piled up with freshly printed agendas for the next school year as well as cardboard boxes with new locker combinations for the new students. Moira sat down next to Diana at the opposite-side from her. Diana looked at Tristan as he left them.

"Alright, we're the lucky team," Vivian explained. "We're doing the easy job while the banners are made, furniture is moved, and books are sorted. All we have to do is take an agenda, put it with the printed time tables for each student, and if they're new or in eighth grade, give them a combination lock."

"Is that supposed to take all morning?" Moira questioned in a dull tone.

"There's more than just this to do, silly. This is just what we're starting with – Mrs. Phillips assured us that there was always extra work to do if we finished before noon."

Moira rolled her eyes and took the stack of schedules that were thrown down the table for her and Diana to sort through.

"Come on, let's just do this and get it over with," Diana said, taking the first schedule as Moira took an agenda.

The two of them go to work, going through their measly half of the hundred and twenty or so students that went to their high school. The others took a bit longer, being only what seemed to be halfway done as they chatted and gossiped more than Moira and Diana did.

"You got to feel sorry for Tristan," Moira remarked out of the blue. "Being split from us, I mean."

"Yeah, I know," Diana sighed, putting the last time table into a planner before scratching her head.

Diana looked up from the table and outside as she noticed Tristan working with the other boys in the classrooms outside of the cafeteria. She gave a warm smile and quiet sigh, seeing him, but it faded as she noticed he was distinctly separate from the other boys. Moira looked at Diana before finishing her last agenda and putting her hand to her chin.

"I got to ask you something, Diana," Moira said as she kept looking at her friend. "Do you like him? And don't give me the bullcrap, like, 'Oh, of course I like him. He's my friend / brother / whatever,' she remarked in a mocking tone.

"I don't sound like that," Diana replied with a frown. "And no, I don't *like* him," she lied.

"Because what happened at the end of last year was a bit hazy. All of the sudden Tristan gets shunned and rumors start to circulate that he's a homosexual after standing up Vivian. You were extremely emotional up to May and not talking to him. I thought you were dating Arturo, but it turns out you weren't. He's in Harlech now, and after your horse competitions, you and Tristan seem to be better friends than we are-"

"How does that make you think that Tristan and I are in a relationship?" Diana questioned, interrupting her.

"I'm not done," Moira said in a strict tone. "It's the proximity and the fact that you smiled more in the last weeks of school than the combined time that I've known you. It was like – it was like you were a completely different person."

"Well, winning a national racing derby can make a gal really happy," Diana replied with a smile as she looked down. "Besides, Tristan and I were good friends before that. Nothing in the spring had anything to do with our relationship, you know that. I told you that I was having trouble with Charlemagne and adjusting – that I was stressful with Arturo and the horse races. Charles didn't want me to race, and I was having difficulty with Arturo. It's as simple as that."

"Is Tristan gay?" Moira asked.

"No," Diana replied. "He isn't."

"Okay…" Moira responded, going quiet for a moment, "then is it okay if I confess something to you?"

"What are you talking about?" Diana questioned, looking at her with the same smile.

"I don't know," she replied in a flirtatious manner as she looked over to Tristan. "I just… I was impressed with those rumors of Tristan apparently beating up Peter, and well, Tristan *is* kind of hot…"

"Excuse me?" Diana replied, poorly swallowing her breath and causing herself to cough.

"Am I not allowed to talk about your brother like this?" Moira asked.

Diana didn't reply and instead continued to look at her. Her heartbeat picked up and her stomach tied itself in a knot.

"I just… I think I like Tristan. And not in the same way as you, as a friend, but I mean, I think I *like like* him. Is that okay?"

Diana made a quiet growling noise and didn't reply.

"Diana?" Moira questioned, looking at her.

"I don't see any reason that I would be against that," Diana said in a gritted tone.

"Do you think he likes me?" she asked, forcing Diana to look at her.

"I… he hasn't said anything to me if he does," she replied, feeling her cheeks redden as she went green.

"Do you think you could find out?" she instantly asked. "I mean, seeing that you're 'tight' as you say. Do you share these types of things together? It seems like you would, right?"

"If there's one thing I know very well about Tristan, it's that he's stubborn to let loose a deep secret," Diana remarked, watching the halls as Tristan left and walked behind the other group into the next classroom.

"Oh good, you're done," Vivian said to the two. "Why don't you go upstairs and help out in the library?"

"Do we get to take at least a break?" Moira asked her in the same dull tone as earlier.

"You're here to help out, not to goof around," Vivian scolded.

"Let's just go," Diana said to her, standing up.

Moira glared at Vivian and stood up with Diana. The two of them left to go upstairs to the library, keeping silent as Diana held an anxious face. They entered the library and joined the other group to help out in sorting books, which lasted for the next two hours and a half until the library was properly organized and ready to be disorganized in the school year to come. The student council supervisor let them leave one they were finished and it was noon, and the pair went downstairs when Diana noticed Tristan leaving his team from within a classroom on the second floor. Tristan held a half-filled water bottle in his hand and smiled as she saw the two coming over to him.

"Hey," Tristan greeted, passing them. "I'll catch you downstairs in a bit. I'm just going to the washroom."

"Oh, I think I need to go too," Diana replied, turning to face him before turning back to Moira. "Pick a seat for us downstairs, will you? I'll be right back."

"Yeah, sure thing," Moira replied in slight suspicion, "but Diana," she added, grabbing her wrist as Tristan left, "you do know the principles of keeping a secret, right?"

"Huh?" Diana questioned, having almost forgotten about the intrigue in Moira's crush. "Oh, of course I do."

"Good," Moira replied with a smile. "I'll catch you downstairs in a bit."

Diana took a step backwards as she watched Moira leave before turning around to catch up with Tristan. Her anxiety resumed as she entered the washroom, the same washroom with a cracked mirror thanks to her. She washed her hands and then walked out, lurking near the boy's washroom as she waited for Tristan. He later exited.

"Hey, how was all that back-breaking labor?" Diana asked.

Tristan looked over to Diana and smiled. They were alone in the corridor.

"You know, it's considered weird to just hang around outside of the boy's washroom, right?" Tristan said.

"It's weirder to hang around the washrooms, period," Diana replied, taking his hand and walking him away from the washroom doors.

"Well, I didn't like it, but it was hardly back-breaking as it was just plain boring. It's over now though. What about you?" Tristan responded to her earlier question.

The couple paused in front of some lockers.

"My task was lame, but at least I wasn't alone. I'm sorry about that," Diana said, bringing a hand to his cheek.

"Don't be," Tristan replied, taking her hand as he looked at her somber face. "Come on, let's go get some lunch before it's all gone.

"Hey, wait, before we go back out there," Diana said, grabbing his hand as he tried to leave with her.

"What is it?" Tristan asked as she brought him closer to her.

"You owe me something," Diana said, kissing him.

The two broke apart quickly from their passionate kiss, looking at each other as Tristan raised a smile at the unexpected sign of romance.

"That felt more like you paying me than I you," Tristan said, smiling at her. "Where did that come from?"

"Nowhere…" Diana replied, smiling back at him before looking down the hall to make sure they were still alone.

Diana then looked back at Tristan.

"I just like to remind myself that you're mine and mine alone," Diana added.

"Of course I am, and you're mine," Tristan replied with a warm smile, kissing her on the check before tugging at her wrist as they started to walk again. "Now come on, Moira is waiting for us and I'm hungry for some pizza."

Act 2, Scene 4

The doorbell jingle startled Charlemagne as he jumped from where he stood, at his computer, preparing to laser through the piece of asteroid debris that Barry salvaged for him. He looked into the transparent hyperbaric chamber where the piece of meteorite sat on a disc in the middle with a red laser pointing down to the top of it.

Charlemagne counted on Mavis to answer to the door as he returned to focus on his work, priming the laser to scan the density and thickness of the alloy to understand its shear strength and the amount of pressure that would need to be exerted to punch through.

A knock at his lab door caught him by surprise again, causing him to remove his goggles and abort his procedure to go to the door. He left his goggles on the table in the middle – the table was moved back as the meteorite was moved out earlier in the morning.

Charlemagne opened his door and saw Mavis on the other side, hands together with a nervous expression on her face.

"Sorry, Mr. Cabernet, but two men… two important men, are here to see you downstairs," she explained.

"Did they say where from. I usually don't take visitors without an appointment," Charlemagne replied, taking off his lab coat and closing the door behind him as he joined Mavis in the corridor.

"They said that they are with the local police," she said in a quiet voice, "but they do not look like they're police constables."

"I'll take a look then," Charlemagne replied, walking into the foyer where he saw two suspicious looking men waiting for him inside. "Thank you, Mavis."

Charlemagne stopped at the bottom of the staircase, letting Mavis leave before walking over to the serious men with unnatural white skin. Each of them were dressed in black suits with black vests, black shoes, black shades, and black fedoras. Their skin was whiter than snow, lips redder than blood, and hair… perfectly hairless. None of them had eyebrows or showed any distinct features to separate them apart.

"Mr. Charlemagne de la Cabernet," one of them said in a deep voice. "Do you have a moment?"

"What is this about? Who are you people?"

"We are simple detectives looking to have some questions answered," the other replied, taking out a notebook from his suit jacket.

"Well, I'd be more than happy to answer any questions, detectives," Charlemagne replied with suspicion, "but in order to do so, I'll need some details into what I can help you with."

"Last night at approximately twenty-three forty-five hundred hours, a meteorite landed in the nearby vicinity in what we understand to be your property. The rock was discovered to be gone within the hour with only small fragments remaining. It is important for us, not only in national, but international security, that you help us locate and retrieve this item."

"Well, I'm sorry, but I'm afraid that I had no idea about a meteorite hitting the earth... Heavens, you'd think I would have noticed."

The officers were quiet as they heard this. One of the men closed their notebook and put their pen back before licking his lips. His tongue was as red as his lips.

"You mean to tell me, Mr. de la Cabernet, that you had no idea about a rock landing on your property during the meteor shower?"

"Of course," Charlemagne replied. "I wasn't home. I was with my friend, Dr. Lambert, at the observatory. There's no better place to be for a meteor shower than in the mountains!"

"You see, Mr. Cabernet, we have reason to believe that this is a solid lie. We have reason to believe that you *were* home last night; that you knew about this meteorite falling, and that you retrieved it out of the curiosity that is well preserved within you."

"Well, I would be glad to hear or see some evidence into these accusations. I am a scientist and expect that as much when I hear outrageous claims such as these. Then again, it is not a matter of science, but of rationalism as policemen such as yourselves should know," Charlemagne replied in a sharp tone. "Of course, what you could have mistaken for me being home is the presence of my two fifteen-year old children, but I doubt either of them would have the capacity or consideration or even capability to do such a thing, which leaves my dear old maid who again, I surely doubt. So officers, if there's nothing more to ask, I suppose that'll be all then?"

The men were silent until of them, the one closest to Charlemagne, brought his white hand to his sunglasses to remove them, revealing his cold white sclera and dark grey irises that looked back at Charlemagne. Charlemagne felt frozen from his stare. The man walked forward towards Charlemagne with his hands together.

"Mr. Cabernet, you're not a stupid man, so let me make this clear to you. You may not know who we are, but we know that you know we're not who we have claimed who we are. That being said, it goes without warning that mutual cooperation is of best interest. Lying to us would not be the smart option, so I will ask again. Where is the meteorite that crashed approximately two kilometers from this residence?"

Charlemagne felt his heart pound. He swallowed his breath and took a deep one in return, straightening his back as he looked at the suspicious figures into their unnatural eyes.

"No lies have been told here, officers. I'm sorry that I am no use to your investigation, but if you need anything else, I would be more than willing to assist," Charlemagne replied.

The men looked back at him.

"Appreciations, Mr. Cabernet," the man simply said in return, putting his shades on before turning around.

The two men led themselves out through the front door, leaving Charlemagne alone in the foyer. He went forward to look through the door window, watching them go back to their black sedan while the other went around to the other side. The other looked back at Charlemagne for a split second before opening the car door, entering, and then leaving.

Charlemagne forced himself from the front door. He started to look around the foyer as if he was being watched.

"Mr. Cabernet," Mavis said, causing Charlemagne to jump in fright.

"Oh, sorry, my dear," Charlemagne replied.

"Is everything alright, Mr. Cabernet?"

"Yes, everything is quite alright, my dear. We're quite fine."

"Shall I make a cup of tea for you?" Mavis asked. "Something to calm you down."

"I would appreciate that," Charlemagne said, sighing. "I'll be upstairs in the lab."

Charlemagne fled upstairs to his laboratory, closing the door behind him and rushing around the room to ensure all the curtains were covering the windows before his ears popped. He quickly went over to the hyperbaric chamber and looked inside. The rock was still where it was. Charlemagne sighed, stepped back and sat down at his stool. He picked up his phone and decided to call in in Barry's phone number.

First, Charlemagne took out the rock from the hyperbaric chamber, pausing his tests for the day as he hid the rock in the minifridge underneath the computer. He then went to turn off the lights of the lab and then exited as the phone rang.

• •

Tristan looked out of his room and into the foyer of the north wing. He held a frown and then closed his door for the night. From there, he went into the gym and through the washroom, which was humid and wet. He entered Diana's room where she was showered, readied for bed and wearing sweatpants and a tank top. Her dark brown hair was messy and wet. The bathroom fan filled the room with a light noise, letting Tristan sigh without being heard as he looked over to Diana.

"Have you seen Charles? I haven't heard him go into his lab all day since we got back," Tristan said.

"I have no clue," Diana replied, sitting down at her desk and beginning to brush her hair.

Tristan gave another sigh.

"Is everything okay with Moira?" Tristan asked her. "She seemed a bit... weird around me. I get the impression that she doesn't like me very much."

Diana straightened up and nearly pulled too hard on her hair as she heard this. She brought her brush away from her hair and looked over to Tristan.

"I don't know what you mean," Diana said, continuing to brush her hair. "She doesn't not like you."

"Are you sure? She acted like I was a nuisance during lunch, and then afterwards, it felt like she didn't want me around. If I'm impeding on your relationship with her, let me know and I'll… leave I guess."

"You're not impeding on our relationship," Diana replied. "She's not going to impede on our relationship either," she added in a defensive tone.

Tristan walked over and sat down at her bed so they were closer together.

"I can't imagine being alone in that damn school," Tristan whined, bringing his legs up as he moved further onto the bed and rested his back against the wall.

Tristan was dressed in shorts and a wifebeater. He also wore running shoes. Diana looked at him with a sympathetic look. She gave a light sigh.

"Moira… she likes you, Tristan," she confessed.

"It doesn't feel like it."

"No," Diana denied in a louder voice. "I mean, 'She wants to have your babies,' kind of likes you."

Tristan looked at her with slight unease and confusion.

"Um, what?" Tristan replied. "You're joking, right?"

"I wish I could say I was, but…" Diana sighed with anxiety

"Oh no," Tristan complained, scratching his head with an anxious look.

"I'm sorry, but it's true," Diana said. "It freaked me out when I first heard it, and now I don't know what to do."

"What do you mean? Why would you do anything?"

"Because I have to! I know that something between you and her is never going to happen. There's no sense in letting her tease herself over something that'll never happen – I've already had to suffer over the fantasy of being with you and know how infuriating it is."

"Right…" Tristan replied.

"God, just thinking about it makes me so stressed," Diana remarked.

"Don't do anything!"

"Then you've got to do something, anything. I've already lied to her by saying that I don't like you and that we're not dating, but maybe that was it. Maybe I shouldn't have said that and I should have just said the truth."

"What truth?" Tristan questioned.

"The truth about us!"

"Whoa! No!" Tristan instantly replied to her suggestion. "You are not telling her about us. Nope. Nobody can know about this, Diana. You know that – I'm not ready for that type of criticism from people."

"Then think of something else, because if it's not something else, then it'll have to be that because I won't let Moira suffer," Diana scolded as she put her brush down and stood up.

Diana went into the bathroom to turn the fan off and then came back to sit down on her bed, facing away from Tristan as she held a saddened look.

"Look, we'll think of something, okay?" Tristan said, putting a hand on his shoulder. "Look at me."

Diana looked back at him with a serious frown.

"Don't be so dramatic about this, please?" Tristan said, bringing a hand to her cheek.

"I don't want this stress on myself," Diana confessed.

"Hey, sometimes stress can be food and can help us find a solution."

"Not for me," Diana pouted, standing up. "I'm going to go make some tea to calm myself."

Tristan took her hand and stood up.

"It's okay, I'll go and make you that tea, okay?" Tristan said. "Just stay here and I'll be right back."

Diana looked at him with a saddened face and complied. Tristan grabbed his hoodie nearby and pulled it down. He then stepped out into the corridor of the north wing to go downstairs.

Tristan walked down to the end of the hall before entering the foyer, going downstairs, and then pivoting to go towards the kitchen. He walked through the dark living room and entered the dinette, noticing a brightness inside the room coming from outside of the mansion.

The brightness was almost mistakable enough to be the moon, but as Tristan walked into the dinette and went over to the window looking out, he didn't see the moon, but a bright light coming down and over the street from above. Tristan tried to see what the source of the light was, but could not see high enough above the street, so he stepped back and decided to investigate by some other means.

Tristan left the dining room, went through the living room, and went to the front door. He opened it and stepped outside, seeing the cylindrical beam of light closer as it shined a specific region over the road like a lamp, but moving sideways with no clear source from above or around. Tristan looked up to be sure there was nothing above in the sky, and surely enough, there wasn't. His curiosity wasn't settled as he widened the door, pulled the hood of his hoodie over his head and went outside. He stepped out and down the steps of the manor, crossing the driveway and going down to the pedestrian gate of the house to get a first-hand view of the bright light. A shimmer was centered in the middle of the circle of light as he opened the gate and left the property.

The distortion seemed to be the source of the light. Tristan looked at the anomaly carefully before stepping forward some more, looking behind him in a brief second-thought, but then deciding to carry on alone… at least for the time being.

Tristan stepped into the pool of light, making his entire body seem as though he was standing in daylight. The simmer flicked as he got close, moving away from him for a second before freezing as Tristan got closer to it. He made his way forward, raising a hand up to bring it into the distortion of air. He slowly brought his arm closer and closer before a sharp pain hit him in the back, sending him forward onto the ground until another hit sent everything into darkness.

Act 3, Scene 1

Diana sat back in her bed, anxiously waiting for Tristan to return. Once half an hour had passed, she stood up to go check where he had gone. Diana looked around for her hoodie, finding it in a pile of laundry and putting it on. She then made her way into the hallway and into the foyer where she saw that the front door was slightly open. She went downstairs and opened the door, stepping outside to see if Tristan was outside, but nobody could be seen in the vicinity and it was dark out besides the light from the street lamps.

"Tristan!" Diana shouted before stepping down the steps of the driveway.

Diana gave a more thorough search before going back inside and closing the door behind her.

"Where the hell is he?"

The rest of the house was dark and silent. Diana went into the living room, dining room, and finally the kitchen where the kettle was cold and the room deserted. The sound of a loud whining could be heard from the garage suddenly.

"What the hell is he doing?" Diana muttered as her ears pointed up.

Diana entered the storage closet and then went into the barn. She shut the door behind her and quickly went down the ladder as fast as she could.

"What the hell is going on down here?" Diana questioned, reaching the bottom of the ladder before turning around. "What are you doing to Zephyr?"

The aisle of the garage was empty, but Zephyr was still whining and stamping in his pen. Diana went over, looking in and seeing her distressed horse thrashing around in the far corner.

"Zeph, what's going on?" Diana questioned. "I thought Tristan was down here."

Diana opened the gate of the pen and stepped inside, walking forward and bringing her arms up around Zephyr's neck to comfort each other.

"Easy, boy, easy," she said. "I'm here. Where's Tristan, boy? I don't like this – I don't know where he is – I don't like not knowing where he is."

Zephyr started to calm down slightly as Diana held him. Deep breaths were shot out from the horse's nose though as he looked forward. The sound of a bucket being turned over and water spilling caused Diana to jerk her head over into the aisle where a cloaked figure in regal red robes had fallen onto the ground.

"Hey!" Diana shouted, letting go of Zephyr and rushing out after the figure as she stood up. "Stop!"

The tall figure froze, straightening out before turning around to reveal itself. Diana's face dropped with shock as she looked at the strange being before her, underneath the robes with a horrifying inhumane face. The being was, of course, not human.

Diana's heart pounded against her chest, filling her with adrenaline through fear. She took a step back with readied fists as she looked at it. Its skin was grey and venous. It had two eye sockets where eyes with no irises, but pure yellow-red sclera, looked back at her. Above the eyes, the forehead was creased with veins shooting upwards. It had no ears or nose, but some sort of (presumably artificial) device attached to its skin where human ears typically exist. Instead of a mouth, its chin sagged down, disappearing underneath its robes. The limbs of the being were a mystery at this point, especially since no sockets could be found in the side for its arms. The bottom of its robe was wet.

Curiously, the being did not continue to stare back at Diana, but instead it immediately dropped down on one leg and lowered its head. Diana's eyes widened as she felt a certain change within herself, causing her to calm down and understand.

"I... I can hear you," Diana whispered. "In my head. Don't be afraid?"

The being continued to remain in position. Diana's hearpace lowered and she felt a bit embarrassed as the being continued to honor her by kneeling towards her.

"Who are you?" Diana asked, causing the being to break its stance and stand up.

Diana got a glimpse at the hands of the being that had spilled out of its robe for a second before hiding back. They were lanky and slim. Its hands were long and seemed to have various fingers (the number of which was unsure at this moment as it hid its hands too quickly). Diana moved her eyes back into the eyes of the being as she felt her heart rate pick up again.

"You're not of this world," Diana said to the alien. "No duh. I still... I can't believe what I'm seeing. I must be dreaming, or hallucinating, or something..."

The being didn't move or flinch as Diana started to freak out, grabbing her head with her hands and pacing around the room. She looked back at the being, twitched and started to focus.

"You don't know what dreaming is?" Diana questioned, looking at the being for confirmation that this is what it had communicated to her.

Diana ignored this question and instead started to go back to Zephyr's stall to close the gate, keeping a minimum distance between herself and the alien being. She looked back at the being and noticed that it hadn't moved and continued to look back at her as it stood still. It was not frozen, but simply in one place with the most patience, looking at Diana.

"You got to help me out here," Diana said. "Give me a nod, or shake your… head, or something. How do I know that these thoughts are not just a product of my own mind? What am I saying… of course these thoughts aren't mine. Still, confirm to me that I'm saying the right things. Are you even talking to me like this? Or am I honestly going crazy?"

Diana looked back at the being for a confirmation, but it didn't move its head and instead continued to look at Diana.

"How can you understand me then?" Diana asked back, looking at the artificial pieces to the side of its head. "You have a translator? How can you understand my language though? There are thousands of languages on this planet, and you just so happen to be able to translate mine?"

Diana waited for an answer.

"You've been around here before…" Diana replied. "No, this is impossible. I'm not believing any of this for a second. You're fake and I'm asleep – that's why Tristan isn't here. This is another nightmare. There's no way some telepathic alien is talking to me right now."

Diana turned her back and closed her eyes. She rested her arms and head atop of Zephyr's gate to hide her fear.

"We do not possess such gifts," a slightly monotonic, angelic feminine voice came from the alien. "If you'd rather, we can make like this, although my translator can only translate so much of my own thoughts and project them back. Our data is limited into your language."

Diana opened her eyes and turned around, looking back at the being one more time as her body shook. She was sweaty and pale.

"I am real, although I am not of this world. I do not want to hurt you, nor do I intend to. Your species dominates this planet, or at least, is your domain, and there are many good words said throughout my species about yours. To us, you are the marvels of the universe even if we do not recognize you as gods as much as special beings, and instead your people sometime regard us as gods. I have seen other species that have dominated in different domains, physical and intellectual, but none were as special as yours. You humans are beautiful creatures, but deadly even as lay creatures you are now. You possess a moderation of physical and intellectual strength, and a specialization into a gift that you do not realize you possess. If such talents were to be realized, it would threaten the existence of other worlds."

"Why not exterminate us then?" Diana questioned. "If we're that much of a threat."

"Some seek to, and those among my species have thought of it too, but since this talent has not been realized yet, or so we know of, those that believe it should be done do not. You do not seem to know what this talent is, so I suspect it is still hidden. Certainly though, your people are gifted with an ethereal gift that will one day be discovered when threatened by extinction. The life on this planet is special – tell me, what do you call such a thing?" the alien asked, raising her hand up to Zephyr.

"A horse," Diana clarified, looking at Zephyr for a moment. "What were you doing to him earlier?"

"Nothing," the alien replied with a bit of fright as she tilted her head down. "I only came out of my own curiosity to see this being while on a separate mission. I did not intend for the being to realize my presence as I was cloaked."

"Okay…" Diana replied, confused at the being's willingness to tell the truth. "What do you mean 'cloaked' though?"

"Like this," the being replied, raising her head as she disappeared and became almost invisible.

A distorted shape was left where the alien stood. The being reappeared and put her right arm back into her cloak, hiding it from Diana.

"I can also disguise myself, but that function has been damaged since I have spilt liquid onto my robe. I can mimic the beauty of your species, but that is all I can do – mimic. You look at me in fright for I am foreign, and this is an expected response. However, understand that I am an avatar of a being, bred from our advanced knowledge to be a vessel for me. I am artificial. I am ugly. I am disfigured. Yet, this form is not even my own. With all the attempts by our species, we tried to change this avatar form, but we could not mimic what the life on this planet has exactly – prioritizing a means by which we could control and be on this planet in physical form."

"I don't know what you just said," Diana replied, "but I've seen a lot of ugly animals in my time at the zoo."

"What is an 'animal?'" the alien questioned.

"An animal is a general term for my species, which includes other species and beings like Zephyr. It's complicated and part of how we categorize the life on this planet. I don't really know the details of it since I don't study biology."

"Ah, I see. Few other beings exist from my realm – only those that we create for our needs. What is this 'biology' that you speak of?"

"It's a branch of science that specializes in the study of life," Diana answered.

"What is this 'science' that you speak of?"

"It's… I don't really know how to explain, but it's basically a term used by people interchangeably with knowledge and technology. Really, it's the process by which we learn things, and I really wish my friend was here to explain these things since I'm not doing a good job at it."

"What is a 'friend?'"

"Seriously?" Diana replied. "It's what we call someone when we like them and they like us. For example, I'm friends with my horse, Zephyr."

"How do you know that your horse likes you? Does it speak your language as well?"

"No, but I can tell that Zephyr likes me because of the way he behaves around me."

The being didn't reply for a moment before asking, "Why do you call this horse 'Zephyr?'"

"It's his name."

"I am beginning to remember how much I appreciate your species – such an interesting species and a beautiful one at that. Names… we do not have personal names. We never needed them. However, your species insisted on giving us names and every time, and I have been called many names."

"Other people have seen you before?"

"Not in this form."

"And how do your own people tell each other apart?"

"Our species does not need to tell each other apart. All that matters is rank. You humans have a strong emotional capacity, I remember now. We do not have emotions."

"You seem to know and display fright though. You were scared that I thought you were lying to me just now."

"I can understand emotion, but I cannot evoke it. I had no fear, but caution."

"Right…" Diana replied with a bit of skepticism, "crap. I almost forgot that I was looking for my friend just now. You haven't seen him, have you? A human like me, but male and with red hair."

"I have seen only one other human, but my partner subdued him before he could place himself in the path of danger. He is safe and we will return him to you."

Diana didn't reply.

"I can sense that he is special to you. Friends... it makes sense – emotional attachments are a part of your intra and interspecies bonds. I must leave now. I must resume my mission."

"What mission? You seem to be wasting a lot of time talking to me. It can't be that important of a mission."

"My partner and I were attacked by members of your own species. We were forced to detach an important cargo, which landed within this region. It is imperative for the stability of our civilization that we retrieve this vessel."

"Cargo? And it landed nearby?" Diana asked.

"Yes."

"I think we have your cargo then. We thought it was a meteorite, a bit of rock."

"Where is it?"

"My guardian – somebody who takes care of me because I'm young and my parents are dead – has it."

"I will let my partner know," the alien replied, pausing for a moment. "I have let my partner know."

"That was fast."

"It is easy to speak with this device on the side of my head. I am telekinetic, and I thought it would have been easier to speak with your species through the mind. I was wrong. You prefer speech. Understandable."

"Right... come on then. I'll take you to see my guardian. He might not react well, but who knows, maybe he knows aliens exist already. It wouldn't surprise me."

"I suppose one more human knowing of our existence is a fair compromise."

Act 3, Scene 2

Tristan woke up to a bright light directly above him. Coldness spread against his exposed back as he laid shirtless on a platform. His arms and legs were restrained by cuffs attached to the hard surface he laid upon, leaving him only above to look up and to the sides where darkness surrounded the circular glass chamber he was inside. A variety of tools and machinery surrounded the table he was kept on, many of which were strange, which inspired more fear within Tristan.

The clamp of footsteps on metal were heard ahead of Tristan, forcing him to tilt his head up, look forward across his body, and towards a cloaked figure who simply walked through what had appeared to be glass, but was in fact some sort of force field. Tristan's eyes widened as he saw a tall man – someone who about six foot six inches with long golden blonde hair, light blue eyes, fair skin, and a trimmed beard. He wore a metal chest plate with a red long sleeved tunic underneath. He was very muscular and wore cargo pants and military style boots.

"Do not be afraid," the man said in a deep, masculine, but monotonic voice.

The clamps around Tristan's arms and legs were released, letting him stand up and back away towards the opposite end of the operating table in fear. The being had knelt down just like the other did to Diana, forcing Tristan to restrain himself from jumping off and running away. Instead, he examined the being closely, noticing his grey robe and large appearance.

"I did not mean harm you, Great One. Please, forgive me."

Tristan looked at the man, breathing deeply as he paused in shyness.

"O-okay," Tristan finally responded. "All's cool. Everything's fine."

The man straightened up and looked down at Tristan. His height caused him to cast a shadow over Tristan.

"I sense that you are confused, but I will explain what you need to know. I am the commander of a grand host that is on an important mission to recover a vessel that was lost and had fallen onto this world. I am aware that your beloved queen is aware of the location of this vessel, and I was instructed to bring you back to your habitat so that you can reunite with her and this vessel of ours can be delivered back to us. It is of vital importance that we receive this vessel of ours."

"Okay, for a start, why are you calling me 'Great One?' Who are you? Where am I? What are you talking about – my queen?"

"I have revealed only what you need to know. I cannot reveal more information because it may endanger yourself and others. I already told you that I am a commander of a grand host. I cannot say where we are. I have been advised that your queen knows the location of an important vessel of ours and that she will take us to it. I was instructed to wake you so that I can return you to her in exchange for this vessel.

"My queen? Diana?"

"Yes, she is the one. I should return you to her so that you can continue your duties."

"Diana isn't my queen and I don't have any duties, but that's beside the point. What the hell is going on?"

"I am to release you. Please come with me."

"Where am I?" Tristan interrupted. "Why am I here?"

"The Great One has many questions…" the man said as if someone else was listening. "Very well, I will explain. Long ago, life began on this planet of yours when…"

"No, not that – but wait, you know how life started on this planet?"

"I am knowledgeable in much, but I can see your distress. You did not ask me how life arose on this planet. Please specify your questions so that I can more precise."

"How did I get in this room? What is this room is," Tristan asked.

"We are inside a quarantine zone aboard an advanced craft. For safety purposes, I had to ensure you were free of any harmful beings that could be a threat to others or myself. I have examined you and determined there to be no threats and gained a better understanding of who you are."

"Well, that's invasive," Tristan muttered. "Why am I here?"

"You had endangered yourself by leaving your habitat with hostile entities around. I was required to act to prevent them from targeting you, which I did by subduing you and bringing you back here."

"How was I in danger? I was walking onto the streets."

"Hostile entities were around."

"Okay… whatever, can I go home?"

"Of course, I must return you to your 'home,'" the man replied. "You seem to know what is of priority, and the priority is the mission."

The man backed off and went through a force field, entering the dark surrounding of the current room.

"Come, let us join the others," the man said, extending a hand to a door that opened as it sensed the man's palm.

Tristan pivoted his legs over the operating table and stood up, feeling strange to be walking around the cold room shirtless, he made his way to the force field and stopped in front of it. Tristan brought a hand up and close to the field but was too hesitant to touch it.

"What is the problem?" the man asked, looking over to Tristan.

"I just… I haven't seen anything like this?" Tristan replied, looking at the force field.

"But this planet is surrounded by its own field. The one before you is not so different, but only artificial and of different composition."

"Is it harmful?"

"No elements go through you. Instead, the area around you simply moves and you slide through without any dangerous particles entering.

"Okay… can I have my sweater back? I don't feel comfortable being like this – it's also cold."

"Sweater?'" the man questioned.

"Uh… yeah, the piece of clothing that was over me? The piece of clothing that was over me?" Tristan explained, bringing a hand to his chest to visualize where it goes. "Are you foreign?"

"Ah, of course. I had to remove your sweater so that I could examine you properly. It was a great privilege to see your human form – as I do not get to see such forms outside of artificial means. It is a privilege to see such physical beauty."

Tristan did not respond to this awkward remark. The man passed through the field and retrieved a tray that held Tristan's hoodie jacket and sleeveless shirt. Tristan went over, took each, and dressed himself.

"Come, we must move," the man said, putting the tray away before leading the way.

Tristan walked behind him, stopping at the force field again before taking a hand through it. The sensation was strange. The barrier moved as he dug his hand through, and the surrounding area pressed down around his arm, cuffing him with light pressure that allowed him to move. It was tight, but comfortable. He brought his entire body through, feeling his hair press down as he made it to the others side before following the alien into the rest of the craft.

"What is this mission?" Tristan questioned the man as they entered a chamber with larger doors towards the opposite end.

A smaller door existed at either side. It appeared to be like some sort of cargo hold with other pieces of cargo, or vessels, which did not look like the meteorite. They were rectangular and smooth-edged.

"I was assigned by my superior to retrieve a vessel that was forced to eject whilst we came under combat by armies loyal to this land," the man explained again. "Your queen, Diana, has stated that she knows where the location of this vessel is, but has requested that we return you to her, so that is what I am doing."

"Okay… she's still not my queen. What do you mean by 'armies loyal to this land?'"

"An alliance of different kingdoms from around this planet have formed an army that attacked my spacecraft. We were forced to eject an important cargo vessel in order to escape. We last saw this vessel in the area near your habitat, and as we went to search, we instead found you."

"What did I do to land myself up here?" Tristan questioned.

"You almost compromised our mission by revealing my partner. In doing so, you would have landed yourself in the crossfire of soldiers belonging to this united army. They are everywhere."

"All I did was approach some light on the street. I was curious because there didn't appear to be any source to this light."

"I thought you could see my partner as she observed the nearby settlement on the other side of the large river of water. I was sure, however, that you did not see those that lurked in the shadows."

"I saw, something – a shimmer."

"You saw a distortion of nearby space by our cloaking devices. It was necessary that we remained unseen as I said."

"How did they not see you?"

"I was cloaked too, and once I had subdued you, I cloaked you as well and brought you here."

The man brought Tristan through a set of larger doors. Ahead of them was another force field for them to pass to exit into the outdoors, but the man stopped and turned as though he had heard something. Tristan looked at him in curiosity.

"What is it?" Tristan questioned.

"We are in immediate danger," the man replied, walking back inside. "Hurry, follow me."

"What?" Tristan questioned again, following the being as he went back through the large doors.

The pair entered a different room to the side and walked through an angular corridor. They then entered another larger room with large bright objects in tubes. Tristan followed the man through and into another room, reaching the opposite side of the craft where large panels with holographic screens displayed an array of bizarre characters.

The man went to one of the devices in the middle of the room, taking a helmet into his hand. The figure of the man began to glitch as if it was a projection, which it was. He disappeared and was replaced by a slim figure in a black robe. Tristan looked at the figure with suspicion. He brought long and slender fingers out from within the robe and lowered his hood, revealing a large head and elongated parietal lobe. He was bald and his skin was a deep grey.

Tristan watched in horror as the alien revealed his undisguised physical form to him. He held widened eyes. The alien brought the helmet he had picked up and lowered it over his head. Tristan took a side step to look at the front of the being's face. The frontal section of his face extended over what would be the coronal section of a human's face, and his occipital bone was larger too. The alien covered his eyes with two eyepieces that rendered him essentially blind.

The ground at Tristan's feet began to vibrate. Tristan looked around in the room as the shaking worsened. He then felt the ground below him rise up, creating a sensation like one was in a fast elevator. Tristan fell onto the floor, landing on his bottom and sitting on the floor like a child as the experience continued. He grabbed a hold of the base of a console nearby, bracing himself for faster speeds, but it never came and he returned to inertia. Tristan opened his eyes and looked around. Everything was calm.

Tristan stood up and took the chance to make his escape as the being was still occupied. He stepped down the corridor, rushing through the ship and reaching the large doors that led out to the outdoors. The doors opened for him, revealing the force field that separated him from the outside, but he immediately grabbed the frame of the door as he looked out.

The spaceship was moving and zipping along and above the surface of the ocean at an extraordinary speed – faster than the Cabernet jet by a long shot. Tristan watched as they roared across the ocean, reaching sunlight. Tristan stepped back and continued along the corridor, entering the next room in the ship, which was the cargo bay, and then another where he came to a type of laboratory with all sorts of different containers and vats. He saw earthly species of animals, small creatures – reptiles and amphibians suspended in viscous fluids – dead. Tristan looked around the room in search of something – a place to hide.

Tristan immediately jumped behind him as he heard the squawking of a tropical bird at him from within a tubular chamber. The bird frightened him to run into the cargo hold again, looking around at the strange containers mounted into the floor. At the exterior side of the room was a large ramp going upwards towards a force field that looked out to the outdoors. Tristan looked over and then fell onto the top of one of the large squared containers as the ship moved up so that he was looking down at the surface of the ocean.

For some reason, Tristan did not move and his body was kept down onto the ground as though there was a gravitational force that kept him steady to avoid entities from falling or experiencing zero gravity. Tristan saw a pair of advanced jets pass over the ocean as the spaceship shot up. The ship then began to spin and shoot off at a faster speed, which created a blur of motion from the outside. Tristan stood up and went back into the lab. He rushed through and into the next room, where there were large and bright tubes shooting up from the ground. Tristan quickly left the room as being near the tubes gave him a headache. He reached the end of the room and the door opened as he got close to it.

In front of Tristan was the alien, looking down at him. Tristan stopped and stepped back, falling over and landing on his bottom again. He looked up at the alien with a frightened face.

"We are safe," the being said, bringing his hood back over his face. "I managed to avoid contact with your planet's defense army and have found refuge in an isolated location of the planet."

Tristan stood up and ran away from the alien. He entered the supply chamber again, ran down to the cargo vessels and then over to the ramp that went upwards to the cargo bay doors. He stepped up and looked out at the vast red desert in front of him. The alien was right; they were in an isolated location. Tristan felt the crisp air as he brought himself out from the force field and stepped foot onto the desert.

The sky was cloudy, but it was daytime. There was a mild wind and in the distance, he could see some wild kangaroos hopping along the landscape. Tristan looked around the land helplessly before falling onto the floor again in defeat. The alien then joined him.

"You are frightened," the alien said, looking at Tristan.

Tristan turned to him and stood up. He held a defensive pose as he looked at the being.

"Take me home," Tristan pleaded.

"I intend to," the alien replied, "but why are you frightened?"

"You're disgusting," Tristan answered, looking at the being. "What the hell are you?"

"I am not of this world, as I have stated. I apologize for the deceit, but it was important to keep the existence of this species' form hidden from those of you that do not know."

Tristan turned away from the being, closed his eyes and buried his face into his hands.

"God, please let this be some sick dream…"

"I will take you back to your habitat if you return into the craft," the alien offered. "However, the craft has taken damage and I will need to repair these damages before we take off."

"Okay…" Tristan muttered. "Just… please don't hurt me, and please take me home…"

Act 3, Scene 3

Diana knocked onto Charlemagne's bedroom door, but there was no response. She opened the door and looked inside the dark room. It was empty. Charlemagne was not home.

"Where is this 'guardian' of yours," the being with the angelic feminine voice asked Diana, looking at a portrait of art in the corridor.

"I… I don't know," Diana replied. "He doesn't seem to be here at the moment."

Diana turned around and looked at the alien in slight embarrassment. The being continued to look at the painting in the hall. Diana's ears flickered as she heard the laundry room door open. She looked out the window and saw Mavis walking across the patio.

"Wait here, I'm going to go ask someone who'll know where my guardian is," Diana said, stepping down the corridor to go to the foyer.

"I will remain here until your return."

Diana left and entered the foyer, looking down and over to Mavis as she held a basket of laundry in her arms.

"Mavis!" Diana shouted to her, causing her to jump.

"Oh," she said, "Ms. Diana – what can I do for you?"

"Where's Charles? Do you know where he is?" Diana asked.

"Mr. Cabernet left for the observatory earlier this afternoon," Mavis replied. "He left after some policemen came to speak with him, and he phoned me not too long ago saying that he won't return until tomorrow morning."

"Damn…" Diana whispered. "Okay, thank you!"

Diana left and entered the hallway going towards Charlemagne's bedroom again. She looked over to the alien as she studied a different painting.

"Fascinating scenes… this artwork is astonishing. You are gifted to have these," the alien said.

"I guess, but listen… I have some bad news."

"What is 'news?'"

"Yeah, I have something bad to say to you," Diana clarified. "My guardian isn't here right now. He's out for the night and won't return until tomorrow morning."

"When the sun rises?"

"Yes, that's what morning is."

"I can wait, but I must warn you that I cannot wait much."

"We're going to get your thing back. Don't worry, just… let me go get some sleep and see if I can wake up from this… weird, weird dream," Diana said, stepping back and turning to leave.

"What am I to do until you regenerate your strength? My species do not sleep in a daily ritual like yours."

"Just wait around – look at some more art, and keep to yourself," Diana replied, avoiding to look back. "I'm really starting to doubt any of this is real. My boyfriend is missing. My guardian is missing. I'm alone, and I'm terrified."

"What is a 'boyfriend?' Is it another word for 'friend,' but of the opposite sex?"

Diana ignored the alien and entered the foyer. She went around to the opposite side of the house and checked Charlemagne's laboratory. It was devoid of life. She then entered Tristan's bedroom and looked around. She went into the gym from Tristan's room, the bathroom, and then her room to see that he wasn't around. She then went back into Tristan's room, closed the blinds and took a blanket from atop of the bed to cover herself with. She then grabbed one of Tristan's pillows and fell asleep atop of his bed.

Some lightening flashed and thunder roared. It had begun to rain.

"This is just a dream…" Diana muttered. "I'm having a bad dream. I'm asleep with Tristan, and he's okay and he's alive. The last four months wasn't a dream – this is the dream. Tristan exists. I exist. I want to wake up."

Diana cried into the pillow and eventually fell asleep after thrashing around for hours, anxiously. She woke up early into the next morning and looked around Tristan's bedroom as light shined through from outside. Diana looked around the room and sat up. She stood up and opened the door outside, grabbing a breath of fresh air before leaving the room and stopping as she saw the alien in front of her.

"The sun has risen. Are you ready to continue the quest, Great One?"

Diana looked at the being and her face sunk. She took slow and deep breaths as she stepped backwards into Tristan's room and sat on his bed.

"No… you're not supposed to be real," Diana said. "What are you doing here?"

"You seem upset."

"I am upset!" Diana shouted.

Diana walked past the alien and went over to the open door into Charlemagne's laboratory. Nobody was there. She then exited into the foyer, went around to the other side of the house, and went to Charlemagne's bedroom. She knocked on the door and then opened it. Nobody was there either. She then went downstairs, into the library and knocked on Charlemagne's study door. No response came. She opened the door and entered. Nobody was there. She then returned upstairs to where she had left the alien.

"Is he not here?"

"No, he's not here," Diana replied in a bitter tone.

"You seem angry."

Diana ignored the alien and stepped into Tristan's room. She then paused and picked up her spirits as she remembered.

"Wait, I can call him! I have Tristan's phone and Tristan has his phone number."

Diana walked out of Tristan's room and went down the hall to her bedroom. She then entered her room and found Tristan's phone where he had left it. She picked it up and found Charlemagne's phone number in Tristan's contacts. She then tapped Charlemagne's phone number and brought the phone to her ear.

"Hello? Tristan?" Charlemagne answered.

"Not Tristan, Charles," Diana responded. "Diana. You need to come home right now."

"What's happened? Is Tristan alright?"

"It's a long story, but the owner of that rock you and Barry picked up is here and she wants it back. They have Tristan."

"My God, is it those dastardly men in black again?" Charlemagne questioned. "I swear, they'll have to answer to my lawyer if they think they can hold Tristan hostage like this."

"What? Wait, what do you mean men in black?"

Charlemagne explained about the visit he had yesterday afternoon that forced him to leave the house and hide at the observatory with Barry. Diana then explained her encounter with similar figures the day before yesterday.

"Look, I don't really want to explain over the phone, but you should come home right now and see for yourself. I just want this to be over because I want Tristan back."

"Of course, Diana. I think it would be best if we didn't make the manor a target, however. I know that these federal agents are lurking around the property. There's been a black van parked near the tunnel under the highway close to the mansion for some time now. Have yourself and our supposed guest meet us in town."

"Uh, bad idea," Diana replied. "How about somewhere a little more private? Our guest would rather not have to meet any other humans – I mean people."

"What?" Charlemagne questioned.

"I have an idea," Diana stated. "How about we meet at the art museum in downtown?"

"Have yourself brought there by noon. I need to buy some time to lose these agents outside of the observatory, and it'll take some time to craft a plan. Have Mavis drive you into town for the time being and see if you can lose the agents outside of the mansion. It goes without saying that they are listening to us speak at this very minute, so I'll be in contact with you by other means."

"Okay," Diana replied, fine. I'll be at the museum at twelve."

Diana hung up and put Tristan's phone in her pocket.

"Where is your 'guardian?'"

"He's in hiding because of some people that want to take your 'cargo' for themselves," Diana replied to the alien. "We're going to go into town and meet him though. Can you disguise yourself?"

"I can cloak myself."

"Then let me get ready, and we'll go into town."

Act 3, Scene 4

Diana looked at the distortion of the alien's invisibility cloak at the steps of the Allabrese Art Gallery in downtown Allabrese.

"Don't you have some sort of technology to make yourself look human or something?" Diana questioned, nervous to go inside with the obvious invisible being next to her.

"Despite my form, I am not a shapeshifter," the alien replied. "I cannot transform naturally, and the device that allows me to project a humanoid appearance has been damaged."

"Whatever," Diana said, walking up the steps so they could get out of sight. "You're just lucky this town is small."

The Allabrese Art Gallery was a large house on the corner of town. It had been converted into an art museum to display various artworks collected from the community. Diana reached the top of the steps of the porch outside of the gallery entrance and opened the door. She then held it for her new friend to walk in before she did so as well.

"Welcome to the Allabrese Gallery," an elderly woman said behind a glass counter in the foyer. "Admission is by donation. Please enjoy your visit."

Diana took out five dollars from her pocket and stuffed them down the glass container where the donations were kept. She then walked past the distortion next to her and went into the next room.

"Let's go," Diana whispered.

The two of them entered the first room and Diana looked into the next to make sure there was nobody around.

"Alright, we can hide here for the next two hours until Charlemagne gets here, I suppose," Diana said. "Where'd you go?"

Diana looked around the room, noticing the revealing shimmer in front of a certain portrait depicting a scene in the central park from over a hundred years ago. Diana went over to stand next to the alien, looking at the painting with little intrigue.

"Such fascinating object this 'art' is," the alien said. "So curious. Such detail."

Diana felt a rush of wind next to her as she noticed the alien move over to another painting, standing in front of it to stare at it. She then went over to stand next to the being.

"Is it because of this 'gift' that you find our paintings so interesting?" Diana questioned.

"No," the alien responded. "It is not because of this 'gift' that your species are able to create such items, but that is not why I am focusing on these items. The *gift* I referred to cannot be described as the capacity or ability to create these objects, although your kind is gifted to create such beauty."

The alien moved away from the portrait and into the next room where some sculptures were on display. Diana joined and stood next to it.

"I see these items your species have created to be in a sense worthless, and yet worth so much more for their beauty. It is curious. I look at these items and it is like I see a captured scene. How gifted your kind truly are to be able to create beauty like the Almighty."

"Well, is it because we're 'emotional' creatures?" Diana grimaced, crossing her arms as she looked at a marble statue in the middle of the room.

The marble statue was of the male form.

"Emotional, and an arrogant species of beings – I have studied your species closely and there is still so much to learn. It is my understanding based on my limited, but extensive observations that this art of your holds such emotional sentiment. Your species claim to the distinct from your cousins, such as your horse friend, and yet when I look at these examples of 'art,' I see differently. It is not a special gift to possess such items, but it is of a talent to evoke what is in these. I have visited your closer cousins and studied your distant cousins, and all have what your species refer to as 'culture.' However, had these cousins of yours held the same level of intelligence and consciousness, only your species would be able to create and perfect what is before us. There is a difference among you, and this difference is attributed to the 'gift,' but the similarity is the cherishing of these items and greater emphasis. Your species and the others close to yours claim to be different from your lesser cousins but are in fact similar. In principle, you are alike on the inside and you express this gift through this 'art' as you handle this origin and anxiety of your existence as a species yearning for more without realizing that there is no more for you. I have observed some of your species seek to emancipate yourselves and become a new being of a higher form, as we have, but misconstrued attempts to achieve such dignity have failed, for good reason. Although your species possess this 'gift,' you, like the lesser of us, possess a curse. The Almighty has provided for you a means by which you can still evolve though, and for that the lesser ones resent your kind even more than they formerly did. Through the Almighty, you have the means to truly become Great Ones. For what I have said though, it would be better if your kind never investigated this gift you possess, for it will bring about calamity."

"Why are we the 'Great Ones?' Isn't your species great too? What's the difference between us and you? You're the ones with spaceships to visit other planets."

"We are not great. My species precede yours, and like yours, we reached a moment in our past lives where we could not evolve anymore without ascending, and so we attempted to and most of us were successful. We emancipated ourselves, but those of us who were successful only succeeded because we did so correctly. We are what your species refer to as 'cold-hearted.' The Host is our life now, and ensuring the Host survives is a necessity. The purpose of life for us is life itself. We accepted this duty, and we made sure to use our intelligence to ensure that life lived on. I have met other species of this fate – one of physical strength, and we enslaved them because that is all they knew of. We made them so that they would become beings of pure strength, and they are now the core unit of our armies led by members of my species. The only other species to reach this decisive moment is yours, but you possess both gift and curse, and there is a better plan for your species."

"Would your species enslave ours?"

"Yes, it would be possible. I would be opposed to such enslavement. Such endeavor would require conflict, and that conflict would inevitably result in my species' existence in a long war. There are members of my species that see otherwise."

"What is this 'gift?'" Diana then asked. "How do you know this 'gift' exists if we haven't realize it yet?"

"We know and have seen it. I cannot say more than that."

• •

Charlemagne drove up the rear of Cabernet Laboratories and made his way out of his vehicle to go out the shipping and receiving entrance. He entered his biometrics into the security panel and opened the door to step inside.

The shipping area was quiet with the sound of a forklift beeping somewhere in the warehouse. Charlemagne snuck down a hall towards a cargo elevator and pressed the option to have him go downstairs into the sublevels. He waited for the lift to arrive, the doors to open, and then entered to wait for it to bring him down to the basement. The lift doors then slid open and Charlemagne stepped onto the concrete steps of the access tunnels and made his way towards another biometric panel that led him into the main laboratories.

The blue shine of Cabernet Laboratories main research areas welcomed him as he followed a yellow line that led him to the end of the hallway and another security panel. After confirming his biometrics, the door opened and Charlemagne entered a large room where the meteorite was being kept in the middle of the room on a platform with a glass cage. Various other scientists were around it, examining it while others worked at computer stations nearby.

Charlemagne made his way down two steps to the main floor of the room before going to the opposite side and up two steps into a protected room inside the lab.

"Stop all testing," Charlemagne said, looking over to Judith in the protected room.

"Charles, why?" she asked, looking over to him.

"We cannot afford to damage the rock any more than it has. Apparently, it belongs to someone and the owners of the meteorite would like it back. They've taken my son hostage until they are given it back."

"What? Who?" Judith questioned, putting her hands on her hips. "What are you talking about, Charles?"

"Never you mind," Charlemagne replied. "Have the meteorite relocated to the shipping warehouse at once."

Judith looked angry at the decision but complied. She set down her tablet in her arms and went over to the microphone.

"Attention everyone, please vacate the space. All examinations have been canceled on the specimen."

Judith moved away from the microphone and towards the closest scientist.

"Contact Facilities Maintenance and have the specimen transported upstairs to shipping and receiving," she said before looking outside as she waited for everyone to leave.

The room thinned out and when the last of the scientists filtered out of the room, Judith took her tablet and walked out of the protected room with Charlemagne.

"Tell me, what's going on, Charles?" she asked. "Who took your son?"

"Diana phoned me this morning saying that one of the owners of the rock was with her. She said that I was to meet with them privately this noon at the art museum."

"Why work with them? Why not phone the police?"

"I do not know who I am dealing with," Charlemagne whispered to her, "besides, this rock may be of more value than we initially presumed. I have reason to believe that law enforcement would be of no aid."

"Why?"

"Listen," Charlemagne said in a hushed tone, putting both hands on Judith's shoulders as the last of the scientists left. "Barry and I were visited by strange men in black suits last night. I am more than positive that they know we have the rock, but we have said otherwise. Whoever these people are, they have authority and have been keeping their eyes on me since the visit. I only managed to avoid them now (I hope). I cannot risk the safety of myself, the children, or the company any longer for this meteorite. I am going to return it to whom it belongs to. I have sent for a car to pick Diana up from the museum and bring her here."

"Perhaps you'll reconsider all of this in the next second," Judith replied, moving away from Charlemagne as she walked with him towards the exit of the room. "My initial scans of the rock have revealed that our suspicions that there are indeed layers going deeper into the object are true. Furthermore, the heat signature Barry picked up persists, but has been in decline. I went ahead to perform an ultrasound on the rock, and... well, I believe there is something alive that is responsible for the heat signature."

"What?" Charlemagne questioned in shock.

"It's a hypothesis, but at the moment, evidence is in its favor. We were prepared to drill into the meteorite to examine its contents further. Studying the dense layers on the outside provides us with a method to pierce through this metal using boron titride. If there is indeed life inside the rock, it could open up many new questions."

"Judith, if there were indeed life in that rock, do you not realize that it would make that life extraterrestrial."

"The first confirmed source, yes," she replied, opening the door for them to leave.

"I'm sorry, but that does not make the situation any better," Charlemagne replied, feeling his phone vibrate inside his jacket.

Charlemagne took it out as they started to walk back to the access elevator, seeing that Diana was here.

"Call your people at the reception desk. Diana is here," Charlemagne said to Judith. "Have her and our guest brought to shipping and receiving. Then, the area cleared and CCTV shut down. Send all of our employees home for all I care. Just have the annex cleared."

"Very well," Judith replied, moving to a phone on the wall.

Charlemagne stopped and waited for Judith.

"Hell, this is Dr. Lambert," Judith said. "Good to hear... has Diana Cambridge arrived her guest...? I see... Yes... Right..."

Judith looked over to Charlemagne, moving the telephone away from her ear for a moment.

"She's alone."

"Send her over anyways."

"Yes, send her to the receiving dock, and have the entire staff clear that area. I am on my way right now. Thank you."

Dr. Lambert and Charlemagne passed into the access tunnels and called the freight elevator. The two of them hopped aboard and closed the doors.

"To think we could have made this company's biggest discovery…" Judith said.

"What could we expect but resistance to the revelation of extraterrestrial life?"

The elevator doors opened and the two of them stepped out. They made their way down the same hall Charlemagne had snuck through, passing the crew who had been given the rest of the day off, and they stopped outside of the closed doors into the warehouse. Judith went to a command console and forced the doors to slide open. She stepped through as soon as some space allowed her through. She then went over to where the rock had been left on a flatbed in the middle of the receiving section of the warehouse.

"Such an interesting shape for a meteorite," Judith said as she walked over to it. "There was not possibly way that it could have been a natural rock."

"Careful with those assumptions," Charlemagne replied, joining her.

The two of them looked at the rock, preparing to part with it until the freight doors opened again, revealing Diana with a security guard. The security guard uniform hadn't changed since last year and was still a ballistic vest, brown collared-shirt, and brown cargo pants with boots.

"Excuse me, Mr. Cabernet? Dr. Lambert?" the guard said. "Your daughter is here."

"Thank you," Charlemagne replied. "That'll be all. Please leave us."

"Very well," the guard replied, leaving.

"And have the doors closed," Dr. Lambert added.

"Sure thing."

The alarm signaling the doors were closing sounded, and once they were shut, it stopped. In that time, Diana walked over to join her guardian and Dr. Lambert by the meteor.

"Diana," Charlemagne greeted, "are you alright?"

"Yeah, I'm okay," Diana replied.

"Where is your friend?" Dr. Lambert questioned. "Charlemagne explained to me that you were coming with someone."

"What? Don't your see that obvious glow next to me?" Diana bitterly replied.

The two of them tried to see what Diana was talking about, but they didn't see anything around. Diana was alone to them.

"Er... there's no one with you, Diana," Charlemagne explained with a bit of concern.

"You don't have to hide. We're alone. You can reveal yourself," Diana said. "Please, before you make me look insane."

Dr. Lambert and Charlemagne's eyes opened as they saw the reveal of a character kneeling down to them. Her head was also tilted down, hiding her face, but her height was obvious and her hands showed.

"Do not be afraid. It is a pleasure to meet you, Great Ones," the alien said in her strained-monotone, feminine voice.

"Oh my God..." Dr. Lambert said, taking a step back.

"You don't have to bow…" Diana said, slightly peeved. "Stand up."

"It is custom to bow before your species," the alien replied, standing up. "To signify that we mean no harm and wish no harm in return.

"You do not have to fear such a thing," Charlemagne said.

"Not fear. Suspect," the alien clarified.

"You have my adopted-son, Tristan, captive," Charlemagne responded. "I only wish to negotiate his return."

"Why do you say 'negotiate' and 'captive?'" the alien replied.

"You've kidnapped him, according to Diana, and want this rock back in return for him. I want to see Tristan beforehand."

"I have made contact with my partner. He is bringing our craft down. I apologize. Our intentions against your son were never hostile, but accidental and for his own good at the time. He was under threat. We will return him to you, take our vessel, and then leave."

"Vessel?" Dr. Lambert questioned. "This is a vessel? Tell me; is there life inside of this vessel of yours?"

"Indeed," the alien replied, "but that life is simply hibernated life and itself a vessel for something that is too complicated for me to explain. Regardless, it is of a royal matter and imperative that we retrieve this and return to our fleet at once."

Charlemagne took a deep breath, looking over to Judith for a moment before nodding.

"We wouldn't want to upset the leader of a species with the technology to explore space, now would we, Judith, dear?"

"No, we wouldn't," Judith replied.

"Nor would we mean to upset, or potentially awaken the Great Ones," the alien replied.

Diana took a deep sigh as she listened to the conversation, shaking her head before hearing a sharp bang against the freight doors. All of them turned to the door, hearing further bangs followed by muffled shouting. Sparks flew out of the door in an arched shape next as someone breached.

"What the hell is going on?" Dr. Lambert questioned.

"We're being breached!" Charlemagne replied, looking over to the alien. "Quickly – hide!"

The alien disappeared as another bang caused the metal cut out to fly forward. The four of them watched as a tactical squad of men in brown jump suits rushed through the room, pointing conventional weapons towards them as three figures in black suits followed from behind. The leader of them, a woman that Diana recognized from earlier in the week, led forward with a badge in her hand as she went to Charlemagne.

"Freeze!" the army personnel shouted. "Don't move!"

"What is this?! You are on private property!" Charlemagne shouted.

"Charlemagne de la Cabernet," the woman said in her own British accent. "You are under arrest under the charges of obstruction of justice, tampering in a police investigation, and harboring fugitives."

Charlemagne looked at the badge of the officer, which was more of an ID card than a badge. He then looked back at her with frustration as the two other agents came around and handcuffed him.

"This is insane! You have no idea of the mistake you're making! The laws you've broken by yourself!" Charlemagne argued.

"We are above the law, Mr. Cabernet," the woman said, looking at him.

Charlemagne squinted at her and began to recognize the woman. The agents pushed Charlemagne forward to walk while the soldiers stood up and took the cargo on the flatbed. The agent started to roll it out. An agent pushed Charlemagne again, causing him to drop to his knees on the ground.

"Hey, stop that!" Diana shouted, moving forward to defend his guardian.

"Diana," Dr. Lambert said, keeping her back and protecting her from the commotion.

"We offered you a chance yesterday to come clean. You refused. A smart man like you should have realized who they were dealing with, but you didn't and now this is the consequence," the female agent said.

"Take him away," a male agent replied.

"I want the cargo secured," the female agent shouted at her troops.

"Yes, ma'am."

"What of the others?" the other agent asked the female.

"Leave them," she replied. "They didn't see anything."

Diana and Judith watched as they took Charlemagne away with the meteor and once it was over, they looked over as the alien revealed herself again and said, "I take it that I won't be getting the vessel then."

Diana looked over to the alien, rolling her eyes, and replied, "Look who just learned humor."

Act 4, Scene 1

"We have to hurry," Judith said to the other two, "especially before they change their mind. Come with me."

"Where are you going?" Diana questioned, looking over to Dr. Lambert as she went to a fire escape door.

"You're coming with me, Diana. It's only a matter of time before they send police or child services to retrieve you with Charles' incarceration."

"That didn't answer my question."

"We have to warn Barry before these agents go after him too, so you're coming with me because if what Charles tells me about you is true, you'll choose me over the authorities."

Diana flinched and felt embarrassed. She nodded and didn't question Judith. She then looked at the alien.

"Come on," Diana said to her. "She can help us get your 'vessel' but we need to go rescue somebody that can also help."

The alien didn't respond and instead followed Diana as he joined Dr. Lambert on their exfil from Cabernet Laboratories. The two of them reached the steep causeway that led into the loading zone and they started to walk up before coming around to the parking lot. The alien cloaked herself as they reached the large parking lot separating the laboratory building from the main road. The remaining two hid behind a car for a moment.

A large, black vertical-takeoff landing aircraft was parking down in front of the main entrance to the laboratories. Several black vans were parked with various agents littered around, some armed and standing guard while people with yellow hazmat suits entered the structure. The rock was removed from the building and brought up the ramp of the aircraft before Charlemagne was forced up the ramp and into the aircraft.

"Come on, my car is this way," Judith said, moving out of cover to go down the aisle of the car park.

Diana joined her and they walked to her car, parked closer to the entrance. It was a distinct dark-red convertible with white wheels – a European import car. Dr. Lambert unlocked the car and looked over to Diana.

"Are you sure your friend will be able to fit in the back?" she asked in reference to the alien's height.

"We didn't have any problem in getting into the taxi," Diana replied, opening the passenger door for the alien to get in.

Diana closed the door once she was sure the being was inside and sitting down. She then opened the front passenger seat door for herself as Judith started the car engine and pulled out. They quickly snuck out of the area, and as she merged onto the highway going back to Allabrese, she sped up to get to the other side of the county as fast as she could.

The drive from Cabernet Laboratories to Nattau Observatory was a long one, even with Judith driving over the speed limit. Sure enough, however, the three of them arrived at the steps of the base of the large observatory. She parked her car on the side of the road and all of them exited to get moving again. Judith led Diana and the alien who had uncloaked herself up the steps to the front patio of the observatory where it looked out to the valley and town below.

Judith turned to the alien and felt nervous about what to do next. She then took a deep breath and simply knocked on the doors of the observatory before waiting with the others for Barry to arrive. Instead, a slit in the door opened, revealing Barry's tired blue eyes on the other side. His eyes opened wide as he saw who was on the other side.

"Judith?" Barry questioned. "What the heck are you doing here?"

"No time to explain," she replied in a rush. "Charles was just arrested at the lab by some sort of special police – they took the rock and I came as fast as I could to get you out of here. They might come for you next."

"Holy hell!" Barry replied, shutting the slit to unlock the door.

Barry opened the door and immediately jumped back as he looked behind Judith to the being that stood next to her.

"What is that?!" Barry shouted.

"Easy," Judith replied, walking forward and putting her hand on Barry's chest. "You remember that wish of yours to meet alien life? Well, here it is."

Barry ignored her and started to shake as he looked at the strange being. She knelt down just as it had for every other human thus far. Diana forced her to stand up as Judith brought Barry into the lab, letting the others walk in behind.

"That thing… it's extraterrestrial?" Barry asked in a hushed voice to his ex-wife.

"Are you okay?" Judith asked in place. "Have you seen the men in black? Charles told me they've been camped outside of the observatory."

"No… not anymore. I can't believe this… alien life on Earth! I have so many questions..." Barry said in awe.

"Now is not the time," Judith replied. "We have to get you out of here."

"Where are we going?" Barry asked, looking at her.

"I don't know – just anywhere but here. I'm still startled by them arresting Charles, and now I've seen to have taken responsibility for Diana. Tristian is somewhere – I don't know where, and our friend is gone with these strange police who have this 'egg' of this thing who is demanding it back. It's a lot to process and I'm having a difficult time!"

"Whoa, just take a deep breath," Barry replied, standing up to go next to her.

"It'll be fine," she replied, taking a deep breath. "Just… let's get out of here before more of those agents show up. Okay?"

"Sure thing," Barry replied, grabbing his coat. "Let's go."

The four of them left the observatory and went back to Judith's car.

"What is the next direction in the plan?" the alien asked before getting into the car. "How do you intend to help me with the mission?"

Judith looked over to the alien as she opened the car door and hesitated.

"What is your mission?" Barry asked for clarification.

"I am on this planet for the single purpose of retrieving the vessel that ejected itself from my ship. I am of the understanding from your Diana that you are here to help me in my mission, so I am asking, what are you going to do to retrieve the vessel from your planet's authorities?"

Judith looked down before over to Barry. Barry hesitated to reply for a moment, but then his face lit up.

"You – I knew it all along. Ever since the meteorite crashed and we retrieved it, I've been searching for where it came from since it suddenly seemed to have just showed up from the skies on the night of the meteor shower. Of course, it was an undetectable ship that launched the rock down."

"My vessel is not a rock. It is an insulated capsule containing life. It is extremely important that I retrieve it for the good of both our species."

"The rock – sorry, the 'vessel' has life in it?" Barry questioned, looking over to Judith.

"That is why I called it an 'egg,'" Judith replied before looking to the alien "but that is beside the point. I'm really sorry, but I'm not the sort that you should be asking for help in these types of things. My friend, Charles, was, but he's been arrested. I'm honestly just looking for myself, Barry, and Diana at this point. Even if we wanted to, we do not know how to track these people down or how to locate the important capsule."

"I am disappointed to learn this from you," the being replied, turning to Diana. "I was promised assistance."

"No, we will help you!" Diana responded before looking at the adults. "What about Tristan? We have to get Tristan back!" she argued, turning back to the alien. "If they won't help, I still will."

"I appreciate the offer, Diana, but I must refuse it," the being replied. "I ask instead that you return me to your habitat so that I can return to my craft. There, you can rejoin with your Tristan."

Diana frowned and then looked back over to the adults. Barry was looking down at the ground while Judith only looked at her apologetically.

"Diana…" Judith said in a somber tone. "I'll take your friend to where it needs to go to return to its people, but that is all I'll do."

"Fine," Diana replied. "Take us to Cabernet Manor. It's talking about Cabernet Manor."

"Okay…" Judith affirmed.

The two of them got in the vehicle. Judith turned on the car's engine and began to drive as Barry cleared his throat.

"On such a note of going back to the mansion," Barry said. "I've been experiencing severe jamming on my equipment in the last month. I'm pretty sure these men in black are the source of the trouble. With a bit of time and the right equipment that Charles might have in his home, I think I could develop a method to track these men in black down and potentially locate your vessel for you. If you'll help me rescue my friend that is…"

"Barry," Judith scolded, looking over to her. "You're not Charlemagne…"

Barry didn't reply.

"I am not too familiar with your communication methods on this planet," the alien replied. "I believe that my partner could assist you once you familiarize him, however."

Judith sighed and continued to drive downhill. Diana showed a bit of relief from her anxiety.

"So, what brought you to this side of the galaxy?" Barry asked in a casual tone.

"What is he saying?" the alien asked Diana.

"What were you doing here – before you got ambushed," Diana translated.

"Our previous mission was a simple pass through your planet with intentions of landing in an uninhabited area to do some research and observations."

"What for?"

"I am fascinated with this planet and its many lifeforms. My experience since touching down in the search of my vessel has been educational. Your Diana has shown me many examples of art, and although I have broken my requirements to avoid contact with your species, your Diana has assured me that it was no peril between our species."

Judith took another sigh, looking into the rear-view mirror at the alien as she hesitated to open her mouth.

"What… what would be the worst outcome if you failed your mission?" Judith asked. "If that vessel isn't returned."

"If I do not return to my fleet with that vessel, the fleet of my species will move in and invade your planet with primary objective of retrieving that vessel. I seek a peaceful resolution to this conflict. I cannot say the same with others of my species, especially those that view life on this planet as a threat to the greater universe. It is my understanding that a war between our species is not beneficial. I do not wish for a war between our species."

Diana looked at the alien as she looked cold in her expression. She thought to herself as she looked out the window and gave gentle nods.

"I will contact my partner on my craft and let him know that we are returning."

"Good idea," Judith replied, looking over to Barry.

"What is that sound that is coming from this craft of yours?" the alien then asked.

"It's called music," Diana answered. "It's coming from the radio."

"Interesting…"

Act 4, Scene 2

Charlemagne was pushed forward by the operatives behind him who continued to point their weapons at him. He was forced down the ramp of the aircraft and into the cavernous hangar of what he presumed to be their headquarters.

The woman in black walked down the ramp next to him, greeting various other agents in the same suave, but plain uniform. They were accompanied by personnel dressed in different garbs, such as lab coats, hazmat suits, and turquoise jumpsuits with hardhats as well as beige jumpsuits and helmets. An agent in the group who was distinct from the other agents because of his physical appearance shook hands with the female agent. He had extremely dark skin and appeared to be of southern African origin. He also was bald and clean-shaven.

"What do you have here," he spoke in a Congolese accent. English was not his first language.

"You got him," the agent said. "Very good, Agent Black."

"He didn't put up a fight, which was a wise move to make. I can't say the same from his other moves."

Charlemagne scowled at them as he stood around with shackles at his wrists and ankles.

"What do you plan to do with me?" Charlemagne interrupted. "You cannot expect to prosecute me – you haven't read me my rights – and even if you lied that you did, I have the best lawyer with the best team of lawyers on this side of the continent."

"And you'll do what?" the male agent replied. "I do not care how many lawyers you have, Mr. Cabernet, because when you are brought to The Hague before an international tribunal, they will charge you with illegal experimentation and crimes against humanity. There will not be much to defend yourself against."

"That's insane," Charlemagne refuted. "I haven't done anything of that sort! The meteorite was found on my property and I am its rightful legal owners – even then, it belongs to the aliens who want it back!"

"Get him out of here!" the male agent simply replied, turning around to join the others as they wheeled the cargo out of the hangar.

The armed agents forced Charles to walk with them, but he didn't stop talking.

"You must know about the extraterrestrial life that is out there! I can't imagine anything else from this suspicious organization! Not to mention your agents who showed up at my house last year after the phantasm invasion! I may not have suspected to have been arrested, but my mind is working altogether to see what this organization *really* is!"

The agents ignored him and stopped in a corridor before the command center. Charlemagne continued to frown as he watched agents walk away, leaving the cargo with him as they waited for an elevator.

"The meteorite doesn't belong to either of us!" Charlemagne shouted into the command center, causing agents and operatives there to look at him. "The aliens came to me asking for it back – it contains life inside of it and this life valued by them! They want it back! You're making a big mistake – I should be helping you! You have no idea what you're doing!"

An agent behind Charles shocked him with a stun baton, causing him to drop to his knees and shout in pain. The elevator arrived as Charlemagne brought himself back to his feet, but he was kept from joining the crew of scientists and engineers from entering the lift with the rock. Instead, the remaining agents stuck around with him. One particular scientist was talking with the female agent, Agent Black, and the male agent.

"I want that rock thoroughly examined," the male agent stated. "I want every possible test you can come up with conducted, and I want a full report as soon as possible!"

"Yes, director, the scientist replied.

"You're making a terrible mistake!" Charlemagne said to them.

"Do I have to give you another tap?" the agent behind him threatened.

"You're going to threaten an intergalactic war if you kill the life inside of that rock – a war with an advanced civilization that has the means of interstellar travel. A war with a species of creatures that are probably responsible for the largest galactic – Ah!"

Charlemagne shouted as he was jabbed in the side with the stun baton again.

"I said be quiet!" the agent behind him said, reeling his arm from Charlemagne.

"Sir, perhaps we should reconsider," the female agent warned.

"No," the director replied. "I want to learn everything that we can from this rock. I want it scanned. I want it cut up. I want whatever is inside of it, pulled from where it hides and examined and autopsied. We can make some major breakthroughs with this specimen, and it is what our client wants!"

"Yes, sir," the female agent replied.

The chief scientist nodded and joined his colleagues in the elevator. The elevator doors then closed. Charlemagne took a moment to examine his surroundings. He looked into the command center, which appeared to be similar to the general assembly of the United Nations in its seating arrangements with computer work stations at each seat and an operative at work. At the front, instead of a podium and grand logo of the U.N., a large monitor with a map of the world displayed itself.

Most of the agents looked alike, with a few minor unique and individual features. The female agent was one of them, and the director was another.

An alarm caught Charlemagne by surprise, triggering the staff to look at the main monitor at the front of the command center.

"We have a contact detected in Sector 6E," an agent shouted. "Small unidentified flying object in our atmosphere moving at about one-hundred-fifty kilometers per hour in Canada."

"Send to intercept," the director ordered. "I want it shot down this time!"

"No!" Charlemagne shouted.

"Are you still here?" the director questioned, looking over to him. "Get him out of my sight!"

Two agents seized him as the elevator doors opened for them to take him away.

"Do not shoot that ship down! Do not shoot it down!" Charlemagne shouted at them, struggling to break free from the grip of the agents.

"Scramble the jets! Prepare a small combat team to secure the crash site!" the director shouted.

Charlemagne continued to struggle, looking over to the female agent who seemed to be the only one in the room who was looking at him with crossed arms.

"Stop! Let me go!" Charlemagne shouted. "My son is on that ship! You can't shoot it down! My son is on that ship! You're making a big mistake! Please, don't let them kill my son!"

Tears flushed down Charlemagne's face as he got more aggressive, wedging his grip away from the agents and forcing another to get involved so that they could drag him into the elevator.

"Let me go!"

The doors of the elevator closed and with a sudden force, the elevator moved down the shaft into the next sublevel where he was then pushed forward and onto the ground.

"It's time we teach you some manners, Mr. Cabernet," an agent said, picking him up and forcing him down a dark corridor.

The four of them entered a room with a row of empty cells. An agent opened the door of the first and pushed him in before closing the door behind him. Charlemagne immediately recovered and stood up to get out, but they closed the reinforced transparent door and left him be on his own as they wandered off.

"Please, get me out of here! Please – don't let them kill Tristan!" Charlemagne shouted, banging his tied hands on the glass.

Charlemagne's voice echoed in the chamber. He began to hit his reddened face onto the glass until he lost the strength to stand and slid down to the floor. They left him alone, and he laid on the floor, crying in solitude and pain.

Act 4, Scene 3

"So, your species don't have names," Tristan said, facing the being in the bridge of the craft. "I need to give you a name – what am I supposed to call you."

The alien had reverted to his human-like disguise.

"You can call me whatever you please to call me if my title does not please you."

"'Guardian' isn't a suitable name. What are some names that my species have called you in the past?"

"I have been given various names," the being replied.

"Name one."

"A name given to me once was Mika."

"Mika? That'll work."

"Very well. I will respond to this name if you call me by it."

The alien turned away from Tristan and returned to his console. His disguise vanished. He brought his hands to his head, removed his hood, and then brought down the navigation helmet over his head.

"I have just received communication from my partner. I am to return to your habitat and reunite you with your Diana."

"It's just 'Diana.' You don't need to add the possessive pronoun. She's not mine – well, actually, she is, but that's not proper English!"

The alien went to the main computer at the front of the spacecraft bridge. Tristan felt the ship levitate upwards and that was all he felt. The craft was silent and Tristan was unsure of whether they were flying or not. Mika simply stood silently at the computer.

Tristan looked up for a moment too look at Mika. Suddenly, the spaceship shook, catching Tristan off-guard and causing him to look over to the alien for a response. He took out all four hands of his and started to move them quickly around the holographic screen of his alien computer.

"Is everything alright?" Tristan questioned, putting his hands on the side of the computer.

"I am detecting an approaching craft from your species' defense army," Mika reported, "but I cannot seem to bring my craft to lose them."

"What?" Tristan replied.

"I cannot flee. If I am to land, then I am to fight for that right."

The spacecraft took another vibration followed by a force of inertia that caused Tristan to fall over. He tried to pick himself up again, but another quake caused him to fall over. The shake was followed by a loud explosion from elsewhere in the ship alongside the scrape of metal.

"I have picked up contact with the local authorities," Mika said, focusing on driving to look at Tristan. "I cannot hold them all back and it is too late to run even if I could."

The lights in the bridge dimmed into a red atmosphere, causing Tristan to worry as he rushed to a safe surface to hold on. He looked back over to Mika and thought he was talking to him.

"I apologize, but I will use what power remains to ensure an emergency landing is as close to our destination as possible. I will then contact you if I am alive."

Tristan looked at the alien as he heard that last word. It caused his stomach to flip.

"What's going on?" Tristan questioned with a nervous voice, fearing the worst.

The spaceship shook again and bounced upwards and then downwards.

"Their power in numbers is too great," Mika replied.

Tristan quickly jerked his head over to Mika as he removed his helmet and tossed it aside. He took a device out from underneath the computer and moved over to Tristan quickly as the craft took another hit.

"We are going to crash," Mika shouted, grabbing Tristan as he touched down a button from a trigger in his hand.

The device emitted a spherical force field around the pair as they were forced to the wall of the bridge through the brute force and speed they were going at.

Tristan closed his eyes only to open them to the site of the hull of the bridge ripping open. The blue sky stared down at the two of them for a split second before disappearing as they were forced in their bubble at the impact to the ground.

The two of them ejected out of the spacecraft and were shot out of the forest they landed in. Tristan closed his eyes again as they hurled through the air, feeling the impact as they split through tall trees before digging into the ground to finally slow down. The forcefield broke as they slowed down dramatically, causing Tristan to fall down into the earth and roll on the ground. A larger explosion was heard in the distance followed by plumage in the distance of the crash site.

Mika helped himself up and looked over to Tristan who was staggering around before finding a tree to stabilize himself on. He looked down and started to cough heavily as he closed his eyes. He then opened them to look down as the ground spun. His knees were shaking and hands trembling.

"I have landed, but the craft is destroyed," Mika said to himself. "You have my location. We will wait here for you."

"Who are you talking to?"

"My superior. She is coming with your Diana."

Tristan nodded and picked up his head to turn around. He looked at Mika who seemed to be fine. He started to walk forward towards the trail of fire left behind by the craft. Tristan went after him, struggling to walk straight as he occasionally brought his hand to the trunk of a tree to help him along.

The two of them walked to the large clearing formed by the crashing of the spacecraft. Tristan didn't realize just how large the spacecraft was until he saw the size of the clearing. Small bits of fire were seen on the side alongside debris jabbed into the land. Various trees had been decapitated and bits of the soil were left as smoldering embers.

Tristan looked from one side of the crash to the other to see the burning remains of the craft in the distance.

"Look above," Mika said as the two of them heard a light sound in the distance.

Tristan looked up but couldn't see anything but a small plumage of smoke alongside three larger streaks above in the air.

"The jet streaks?" Tristan questioned.

"No, the additional one."

Suddenly, a vertical-takeoff aircraft flew over the two and the trees beside them. It hovered over the clearing of the land before getting close to the crash site to set down.

"I've seen that type of vehicle before…" Tristan said. "On the night of the meteor showers… it was out searching in the fields."

"We must leave," Mika requested, stepping back as the ramp of the vehicle extended outwards and the rear door opened.

"Disguise yourself," Tristan suggested.

"I cannot," Mika replied. "My abilities were damaged in the crash."

A small team of six men and women in brown jumpsuits armed with strange weapons started to run down the ramp, securing the landing zone before standing up to face the wreckage in the distance.

"I don't think that's good," Tristan said, looking over to Mika who had disappeared into a vague distortion of the air around.

The craft was extremely close and some of the soldiers had started to tactically make their way around the side to secure the crash site.

"We need to leave. The planet is of your species, so lead me," Mika said.

"Okay…" Tristan replied, moving away and going back the way they came.

Act 4, Scene 4

Charlemagne sat in a lone chair in his cell with his head down until he noticed the appearance of two agents outside of his cell.

"Charlemagne," one of them said. "Our agents in the field converged on the location of your friend, Dr. Bartholomew Lambert, but were unable to find him. The observatory where he resides was found empty. Do you care to share any intel on his location?"

"The alien craft... did you shoot it down?" Charlemagne asked in return in a weak voice, ignoring their questions.

Both agents looked at each other before looking over to Charlemagne with neutral expressions.

"The unidentified flying object seen over Canada was shot down with three missiles tipped with nuclear warheads. Strike Team that responded to the crash site has reported there to be no survivors."

"No..." Charlemagne muttered, closing his eyes and digging his face into his hands.

"But here's the thing, Mr. Cabernet. We're in charge of Earth's defense, but people like yourself and your friend Dr. Lambert stand in the way of the safety of the rest of the world. If you really cared about doing what was right, you would be helping us instead of assisting foreign forces."

"Go to hell," Charlemagne interrupted. "I won't assist you."

"It is vital that we find Dr. Lambert, Mr. Cabernet. His life depends on it."

Charlemagne didn't reply and continued to look down as he removed his hands from his face.

"What was he researching in relation to alien life?" the other asked.

"What do you know about extraterrestrial lifeforms? Do you know where we could meet one?"

Charlemagne squinted and glared at the ground. He then stood up and looked at the agent, confronting them.

"I do, but here is what would happen if I were to reveal anything about these lifeforms. You would hunt them down and have them killed. You would arrest them and instead of attempting to communicate with them, you would torture and leave them for dead to pick at their bones. That is the organization that is here does – it is one of efficiency at whatever cost and total disregard for life itself. It does not care about truth, but about reaching its end, which I can only know to be selfish."

Both agents were silent. They turned around as another agent entered the detention center.

"What are you doing here? We are conducting an interrogation."

"I understand," Agent Black replied, "but I am relieving the both of you from that duty on the orders of Director Selebi. I will handle this from here."

The agents glared at her before looking at Charlemagne with the same nasty eye. They left without any resistance and wandered off. Charlemagne looked at the woman as she maintained her hands at her hips until they passed her, triggering her to cross her arms until she knew they were gone for sure.

Charlemagne glared at her as well and slammed his hand on the hardened glass.

"My son is dead because of you!" he snarled.

"If that is true, then I am sorry for your loss," she replied. "Our crews are working on salvaging the wreckage of the UFO near Allabrese, and while they may not have found any survivors, they also did not find any corpses."

"What do you want from me? I have little to say to you as I did with your pawns."

"I am not here to question you, Mr. Cabernet," she said, swiping a key card into the computer.

Charlemagne's cell door opened.

"I am here to release you on certain conditions."

"And what is that? Charlemagne replied, stepping out as he looked at the woman.

"Do you remember me?"

"How couldn't I? You broke into my house and threatened me."

"I am Agent Eleanor Joan Black, member of the Global Defense Project, an organization that concerns itself with the unknown to protect the public from the unknown, and to mask secrets that would be too damaging to the status quo and balance of power across the world. Some people like the way things are on our planet, and we are in place to ensure that remains as it is."

"So, you're the global anti-change group."

"Seventy years ago, the world was forced to handle its power with the largest and deadliest weapons known to us taking thousands of innocent lives. We entered a new era, but we got through it and would like to ensure that such anxiety is never forced upon us ever again in such a sudden manner. Change is good, in my opinion, but the world does not need such sudden change. We ensure that sudden changes are dealt with, if not avoided."

"Why are you letting me go?" Charlemagne simply and quietly said next.

"Because I need your help. You see, you were right about shooting down the UFO and I fear that you are right about the contents of the meteorite. Less than ten minutes after shooting down the spacecraft, our radars detected a large mass of objects orbiting above the Pacific Ocean. I've lost complete confidence in this organization, and so, I am defecting along with several other crew members who I trust. Our director… he has betrayed his mandate on the basis that we have no choice but to fight the aliens. I disagree. We intend to hijack our second V-TOL shuttle and leave. I am offering you an opportunity to leave with us because I know that you will be valuable to the cause. I know you, Mr. Cabernet, even if you've just met me. You are intelligent and are of high morals. Our leadership in this organization has neither."

"How do I know this isn't just a ploy to get to Dr. Lambert?" Charlemagne asked.

"A reasonable observation, I suppose… this is not a honeypot. I don't care if you take me to Dr. Lambert. You assume that you have a say in where we will establish ourselves or what we will do. Our primary mission henceforth is de-escalation. In order to accomplish that, we must petition The Committee to terminate the leadership of Director Selebi."

"Okay… I can aid you then. Anything to stop a global war."

"Good," she replied, extending her hand to Charlemagne's. "We have work to do, and it starts with getting ourselves out of here."

• •

Judith pulled into the driveway of Cabernet Manor. All four of them left the vehicle as soon as the engine shut off and they all made their way into the mansion.

"Charles has a pickup truck in the garage," Barry stated. "We can use it to rescue them."

"Follow me then," Diana replied, rushing through the house and going into the kitchen.

Mavis appeared to be out of the house as it was quiet for the Tuesday evening that it was. All four of them got to the freight lift in the storage closet and were brought down to the garage where Zephyr rested.

Barry got the keys for the pickup truck from the cabinet, opened the doors for them to enter from the outside, and then went to the pickup truck. Diana hopped in the back and noticed Judith to be staying back.

"Carry on without me," she said as the alien was brought into the front cabin.

"Alright, wait here," Barry replied. "If you see the men in black…"

"I know what I'll do if I see them, Barry…" she responded. "Just hurry…"

Barry nodded to her and shut his door. He then started the engine and watched as Judith went to open the shutter doors. The pickup truck drove out and through the dirt pen before getting to the gates. Diana hopped out to open them before getting back into the truck. The tree of them drove through the field behind Cabernet Manor and went all the way to the stream below a small ridge that went into the dense forest uphill of the Rocky Mountains.

"I sense them to be further along this way," the alien said to Barry as they got to the cliff.

"Alright."

Diana felt her heart pumping as she sat back with anticipation to see Tristan again. The truck drove down the ridge until it came to a halt as the being told them that they were extremely close. Barry got out of the car, prompting Diana to hop out and join him as they went to get a better look around.

At the edge of the creek, Diana saw Tristan down by the water, alone. Her face immediately turned to a smile, causing her to run along to get a better angle for her to hop down onto the rocks by the water. She then rushed over to her other half. Tristan turned his neck as heard her footsteps in the rocks.

"Huh?" he questioned, smiling as he saw her.

Diana brought her arms around him and embraced him.

"You're alive!" Diana whispered as she hugged him. "Thank God, you're alive."

"Somehow…" Tristan replied in the same hushed tone. "… Are you crying?"

"I just… I missed you and was scared," Diana replied back, wiping her eyes in his shoulder.

The couple soon parted as the others joined. A cloaked alien revealed herself next to her. Mika knelt down from atop of the rock he stood on and bowed his head down.

"Do not be afraid, Great One."

"This is Diana, Mika," Tristan said.

"Oh great, yours does that too…" Diana remarked. "Why do you call him Mika? I thought they didn't have names."

"I named him," Tristan replied, causing Diana to roll her eyes.

"Is everybody okay?" Barry shouted as the other alien made her appearance next to him.

"There she is," Mike said, standing up to face his superior.

The alien moved off the rock and started to make his way up the ridge to rejoin the other two. Diana and Tristan followed from behind.

"I apologize for crashing your craft," Mika said to the other.

"No need. I am sure you have sensed what I have sensed too since the crash."

"I have, and I fear that it is too late."

"It's not too late, guys," Barry replied.

"Great One, I thank you for taking care of my master," Mika said, kneeling down.

"You don't have to keep kneeling down," Tristan said. "Let's just go."

"Certainly," Mike replied, standing up as they made their way back to the car.

• •

Diana kept a hand at Tristan's wrist as they drove along the field back to the mansion. Barry drove through the pen and into the garage where Judith seemed to have left. Tristan and Diana got out of the back of the truck, and Diana opened the door for the aliens to get out while Tristan closed the shutter.

"So, what's next?" Diana asked as they made their way to the elevator.

"I don't know," Barry replied to her.

All five of them boarded the lift and were brought back up. They made their way to the foyer where Judith was sitting down near a window looking outside.

"Oh, good heavens, you're back," she said, standing up and going to them.

"Peace be with you," Mika said, kneeling down.

"There's two of them?" Judith questioned.

"Your peer here was telling me how we may communicate with the defensive organization that stole your Charlemagne," the female alien said, "but I am afraid that such action would be pointless."

The house started to shake with the sound of a loud rotor passing over the house.

"Oh no," Judith expressed as everybody jerked their heads to face outside.

Dr. Lambert moved to the front door and looked out at the V-TOL touching down on the street.

"Let's go," Barry suggested, taking Judith's arm.

Judith shrugged him off.

"They've blocked off the road."

The aliens immediately cloaked themselves, triggering Diana and Tristan to look over to the distortion of space where they stood.

"There's still time," Barry whispered to Judith. "I can go around."

Judith was quiet as she looked at the ship with its rear door opening and ramp touching down.

"Fine," she replied. "Go and I'll buy some time."

"You got it."

Barry got away from the door and looked over to the others for them to join him. Judith opened the door as soon as she couldn't see them anymore. All of them got to the truck and Tristan opened the doors before hopping into the back. Barry hesitated to step on the peddle for them to get out, but he did it eventually. The truck launched out of the garage, through the mud pen and around to drive onto the road for them to escape.

"Where are we even going," Tristan whispered in disillusion.

"I know… it feels like we're at the end of everything," Diana replied as the car hit the road.

Diana poked her head up as she noticed who was at the base of the ramp of the V-TOL.

"Hey, Barry! Wait! Turn around!" she shouted.

"Huh?!" Barry questioned, looking into the rear-view mirror.

Dr. Lambert stepped onto the brakes. He saw in the rear-view mirror Charlemagne hugging Judith at the base of the V-TOL ramp. He immediately turned the truck around and started to drive back. Charlemagne and Judith weren't alone. With them were three men and a woman in a brown jumpsuit. There was also a woman in black. Barry brought the car back and drove it towards the aircraft. He stopped in front of it and shut off the engine. He then looked at his best friend with a smile as he got out.

The kids hopped out of the back and Diana let the aliens out before going over to Charlemagne. Charlemagne's expression dropped in shock and surprise as he saw Tristan.

"You're alive!" Charlemagne said with a smile across his face. "I thought you were dead!"

"No, but as advanced as these alien spaceships are, they have a serious lack of seatbelts," Tristan replied.

"Charles," Barry greeted as he joined the others. "What's going on? Who are these people? I thought you were arrested."

"I was, but I made a deal with some of their smarter members, and here I am now," he explained. "Barry, this is Agent Eleanor Black. She's in charge of these people."

"Dr. Lambert," she replied, shaking Barry's hand.

"Pleasure to meet you."

Diana and Tristan stood with the aliens who had cloaked themselves.

"Diana, where are the aliens?" Charlemagne asked.

"Right next to us," Diana answered. "You can show yourselves."

The cloaks of the aliens faded as they revealed each other to the newcomers of the small crew.

"You don't have to kneel," Diana muttered to her companion.

"Apologies."

"So, these are our little green men," Eleanor remarked.

"Are you here to help us in our mission," Mika asked.

"Mission?"

"We are here to retrieve our vessel that crashed down in this area of your planet," Mika explained once more.

"You took our vessel," the female added. "I recognize you from earlier."

"I did take your 'vessel,' but it's in the hands of my superiors. I am here to help you get it back."

Agent Black started to explain her side of the last two days. She told them about who she formerly was in the Global Defense Project, and that a war between each species was pending with the arrival of alien battleships over the Pacific Ocean.

"It is as I feared. War is inevitable," the female alien said.

"What are you talking about?" Charlemagne questioned.

"I do not wish to explain in detail, but our species are not in this sector of the galaxy by chance. We are here to conduct surveys on the current status of the planet and the progress of your species. You see, your species holds a gift unlike anything any species has ever handled or been able to handle. It is our understanding that if this gift were to be discovered, your kind would be an unstoppable force due to your reckless capacity of emotion that you refuse to shed. Some within our species view you as a threat that need to be exterminated while others such as myself see you as people that will never discover this gift together but may be inclined to if thrusted into a war that threatens your survival. Both of us agree that it is too late to stop you with the point of technology you are at now, but I believe that all we can do is to stay back and stay away. If the fleet is here, then the failure of my return has prompted the military council to take control and prepare for war."

"Then we don't have much time to lose," Eleanor remarked.

"The downed UFO could serve as a motivation for this civilization to declare war. It is a major concern that we could take down such an advanced craft with our technology," Charlemagne explained. "It could elevate their concerns about us as a threat."

"What about the vessel? Does it matter if we retrieve it?" Eleanor questioned.

"The vessel contains life that is important to us and must be returned," Mika argued.

"I can help you with that objective, but you must tell me how you can guarantee peace with us," Eleanor asked in return.

"With some more assistance, I would need to return to our fleet and speak with the council," the female alien requested. "I will require a form of transport, one that I do not believe your species possesses. What will you do to secure our vessel?"

"I will secure your cargo, but in order to do so, I need to infiltrate the G.D.P. headquarters. It won't be easy, but it can be done."

"Then it's settled," Barry replied. "We have a plan of action."

"The idea of one," Eleanor corrected before taking a deep breath and looking down. "We cannot stay in Allabrese. The director has probably dispatched half of the organization to come here and look for me with Charlemagne. Besides, we have nothing in terms of resources or equipment to do anything of the sort that we wish to do."

"Leave any of that to me," Charlemagne said. "Equipment, resources, manpower... I can provide whatever it is that is needed, and I believe that I know the perfect location for us to go to."

"What's that?" Eleanor asked.

"A small facility of mine in the interior of British Columbia near town of Kennte."

"Very well," Eleanor replied. "Let's move there at once."

"What's going on?" Moira asked, hopping of her bike as she stopped in front of the pickup truck.

Everybody turned to face her, including the aliens who knelt down at her sudden appearance.

"Bring the girl," Eleanor simply said.

Act 5, Scene 1

Charlemagne watched from within the cockpit of the V-TOL aircraft as they raced over the white summer clouds, flying west towards the setting sun. It was almost twilight, but everybody was alert with urgency.

"I wasn't aware that Cabernet had a space facility," Eleanor remarked as she piloted the aircraft.

"I'm allowed to have some secrets from the world governments, aren't I?" Charlemagne replied.

"Hmm..." she responded with displeasure. "We're getting close. Everybody hold on as I make our descent."

"Already?" Diana questioned as she sat between Moira and Tristan in the cargo hold behind the cockpit.

"We're not in a helicopter," Barry explained from the bench across. "We're in a high-tech vertical-takeoff and landing aircraft with jet engine propulsion. If I had to guess, DARPA was the source of this craft.

"DARPA would be jealous to have a craft like this," Eleanor replied as she steadied her hands on the controls. "Charlemagne, take the co-pilot seat. I'm diving in five."

"Five minutes?" Charlemagne questioned, sitting down and putting on his seatbelt.

It wasn't five minutes. Eleanor quickly turned the craft to the right, taking the ship down and into a J-turn as they went past the white plumage of clouds in the sky. They came into the long desert where a small town stood ahead of them.

"Did you get your answer?" Eleanor asked as she slowed down and approached the town.

Charlemagne looked over to her unpleasantly as she held both hands forward onto the dashboard ahead of him.

"Just take the radio and warn your people that we're making out approach," she replied.

Charlemagne looked over and found a radio to pick up. He brought the mouthpiece under his nose and started to fiddle with a dial to find the right frequency to communicate with the space station.

Eleanor flew over the town meanwhile, going past it and over the Kennte River that ran beside it.

"Control, this is Charlemagne de la Cabernet making my approach to the Cabernet Outpost. Do we have access to land?"

"Mr. Cabernet, please identify yourself," the radio replied.

"Vienna," Charlemagne answered. "Romeo-Victor-Echo-One-Hotel-Two-Seven-Whiskey-Sierra-Juliet-One."

"Thank you, Mr. Cabernet. You are cleared to land."

"Thank you," Charlemagne replied, putting the radio back.

Eleanor dragged the ship up and brought it to the sharp hills besides the highway. They went towards a small base in the center of the plateau ahead.

"It's smaller than I expected it to be," Eleanor observed.

"It will provide us with what we need."

The V-TOL crossed the desert and started to touch down as it approached the runway leading to a large hangar at the end. The facility was small. The mud-green hangar doors were closed, hiding whatever existed inside. Next to the hangar was a two-story annex with beige walls and tinted windows streaked across. A road branched from the runway and passed in front of the building, going forward, all the way to a checkpoint before blending into the desert road out of the facility. Before the checkpoint, the road connected with another road perpendicular, which went down and in front of the two warehouses and three-story office complex before connecting to another perpendicular road that ran parallel to the previous one, connecting to the runway at the bottom. In the middle of these roads were some barracks and portable structures.

Eleanor drove the V-TOL towards the annex of the hangar where she saw a helicopter landing pad. She slowed down and hovered there. She then brought the craft down, giving herself and Charlemagne a view over the complex. Charlemagne looked at the runway, seeing the extension of road at the very end. Although it was a runway for cargo planes, it was also the track leading to the launch pad a couple of kilometers from the facility, which could be seen in the rough and flat sandy landscape.

Charlemagne unlatched his seatbelt and stood up, turning from his chair and going down the steps leading into the cargo hold. The rear door of the V-TOL opened up and everybody else stood up to leave as a burst of warm air rushed through the interior of the craft.

Everybody left the vehicle and stepped down into the shade under the rear tail of the V-TOL. An elevator shaft to the side of the roof opened, revealing a small team of scientists led by an elderly man. He had fair skin, medium-length grey hair combed back, and good posture. He stood out from the others by his age and his civilian dress – he was dressed in a black suit. The other scientists did not wear lab coats, but were dressed in cargo pants and green Cabernet Space sweaters that were sharp and had zippers at the top quarter

"Mr. Cabernet," the man said in a South African accent before pausing as he looked at the two lanky and tall beings that stood behind the group.

"Stop," Diana said, tugging at the robe of the female alien as she started to kneel.

The scientists started to mumble to themselves as the knees of their team lead shook and his eyes were wide.

"Is that..." the man hesitated.

"Yes, it is alien life," Charlemagne said. "And I expect you five to be last five to learn of their existence. I will explain later, Dr. Brown, but until then, we need to get organized to prevent a global catastrophe. Is the Lindworm ready for launch?"

"No, we are only in phase three of the program. We are having difficulties with its design, sir," Dr. Brown replied.

"Well, then we are going to have to accelerate its development with my help," Charlemagne responded.

"My help too," Barry added.

"What is this 'Lindworm?'" Mika questioned.

"Lindworm is the name of our spacecraft," Charlemagne explained. "We need to finish her development before we can launch you to your people."

"If you would prefer, I could assist you in any way I can. In addition to piloting experience, I am deeply knowledgeable in the design of our crafts."

"We will need all the help we can get," Charlemagne replied. "Eleanor," he added, looking to Agent Black, "what will you need for the mission."

"Men," she replied. "I only have four."

"Count me too," Diana insisted.

"Diana, no," Charlemagne rejected.

"I can handle a gun. You know that," Diana countered.

"It is too dangerous."

"Charles, you said it yourself that we will need all the help we can get," Eleanor remarked. "If war breaks out, the children of all ages of this world will come under an even greater danger. So, unless you know of some local mercenaries, we will need you to take whatever we can get. Of course, that reminds me – the personal army you asked your people to form after the events in Egypt is not ready. So, we very much will need Diana's help as well as Tristan's and Moira's."

Charlemagne didn't reply. Instead, he cleared his throat and looked over to the aliens.

"I have thought about the proposed mission ahead of us and decided to join the team that will recover the vessel," Mika said. "It is my duty to protect this vessel, and it will be my duty to ensure that it is recovered."

"You will leave me to go to the fleet then?" the female alien replied.

"I will provide you with an escort team – I can offer two of my soldiers to go," Eleanor replied. "Captain Poulsson and Sergeant Zajaczkowski."

"These people are not enough for the Lindworm," Dr. Brown cut in. "You will need at least a fourth."

"We don't have enough people to expend. Charles? Dr. Lambert? Do any of you care to volunteer?"

"Barry, this is your opportunity to go into space," Charlemagne said to him.

"Huh?" Barry replied, looking over to his friend. "It is… but I'm not fit enough to go up. I won't make it."

"Let me go then," Tristan offered. "I don't even know if I'm fit enough, but we can find out, can we?"

"Tristan…" Charlemagne said with a sigh.

"Charlemagne," Eleanor replied. "We have no other choice."

"Very well," Charlemagne affirmed. "Dr. Brown, I'm entrusting you with their training. Take care of my son and make sure he is fit enough for this mission."

"Yes, Mr. Cabernet," Dr. Brown replied, bowing his head.

"You best go now," Eleanor said, looking over to the doctor.

"If you'll kindly follow me then," Dr. Brown said, noticing the alien to not be following him.

Dr. Brown did not care and instead entered the lift with Tristan and the two operatives.

"One more thing, doctor," Charlemagne said, turning to him. "Have the entire compound evacuated and the remaining staff sent home. No one can know of what is going on and no one else can know of the extraterrestrial life here. Understood."

"Of course, Mr. Cabernet," Dr. Brown replied, bowing his head once more.

Diana looked over to Tristan with a worried expression and the elevator doors closed.

"Alright, you have your astronauts. What else will you need to infiltrate your peoples' headquarters?" Charlemagne asked with a bitter voice.

"I'm not sure. I don't know how I'm going infiltrate it yet. With our defection, they'll change the security layout for sure," Eleanor said, looking over to Moira, "but of course, any security that's part of their system will be obsolete if we have our eyes on the inside."

"I met this girl with your daughter about two days ago after she tried to – after she did hack into our system through a port in one of our vans. She did it once, and I'm sure she can do it again."

"I can't do that again," Moira rejected. "I mean, it's more complicated than just logging into any ordinary computer. I also got lucky with you because you left a port so exposed in the open like that."

"I can help her then," Judith said. "I know more about computers than anyone else here."

"If I gave you the details of our communications, do you think you could hack into that too?" Eleanor asked.

The screech of a public announcement system cut them off.

"All personnel, this is Chief Engineer Dr. Elias Brown initiating Emergency Evacuation Protocol One. All staff and security are to leave the premises at once as soon as possible. I repeat, we are under Protocol One. All staff are to leave immediately until further notice. Compensation will be provided to staff for missed time. All personnel are to refrain from entering the premises until further notice."

Judith waited for a moment before looking back to Agent Black.

"I could," Judith said.

"I am knowledgeable in encryptions and codes. Our species use a similar, but more advanced system in our electronics. I could assist and provide consultation in this endeavor," the female alien stated.

"Very well," Eleanor replied. "Do you have a space for these ladies to work, Charles?"

"I believe the operations center in the main building should be vacant. It will have all you might need," Charlemagne explained.

"And what about my team?" Eleanor said, walking over to the elevator. "I'll need a space to train and plan this operation. Does this facility of yours have any sort of armory? Perhaps a security complex?"

"I believe so," Charlemagne said to her. "There is an armory in one of the warehouses used by our security team."

"Let's get moving then," Eleanor said. "We don't have much time to prepare. What will we do about living arrangements?"

The rest of the group entered the elevator.

"There are barracks and a cantina. I'll see about having some of the kitchen staff working to keep us fed. However, that'll mean keeping some security officers around to keep an eye on them. I'll be sure that CCTV is shutdown so that they don't catch the aliens. We should be sure that we don't let be on their own."

The elevator came to the ground floor. The doors then opened and they stepped onto the pavement next to the road at the base of the structure. There, there were four jeeps parked for them with Dr. Brown and his team standing around.

"Mr. Cabernet, the facility is evacuating as I speak. I've had these cars brought for us as well."

"Thank you, doctor," Charlemagne replied as his team boarded a car. "Doctor, have some of the kitchen staff remain as well as some of our security team. I want CCTV disabled and special instructions given to these staff who remain that they are to stay out of certain areas. Security are to monitor the outdoor perimeter and report any intrusions."

"Yes, Mr. Cabernet."

Diana went over to Tristan before he boarded his car. Tristan looked at her as the others organized into the other jeeps.

"Be careful," she said to him.

"You too," he replied.

Diana watched as Dr. Brown drove off with the astronauts-to-be, leaving her with Eleanor and the two other operatives as Charlemagne and Barry took another jeep with Mika with the other engineers. Judith and Moira boarded another with the remaining engineers and the female alien. All of them split up, leaving them to prepare for the mission to come.

Act 5, Scene 2

Agent Black parked the jeep outside of the warehouse she was told to go to by Charlemagne. It was a tall indigo building with windows across the upper levels of the wall and large doors below with a smaller one to the side.

Eleanor and the two other agents had settled themselves inside a warehouse with Diana. It wasn't as big as it looked on the outside. It comprised of four aisles with a small space at the front entrance and main doors. Eleanor commandeered a table where the three of the agents had laid down all of the gear they had collected in the last hour. It wasn't much, but it was all they had.

Amidst the armory, several low-tier assault rifles, ballistic armor, and other gadgets were stored in lockers and shelves. Eleanor threw a jumpsuit down onto the table and looked at Diana.

"You're no good to me dressed like a civilian. Your comfort is something you'll have to abandon if you're to come with me on this mission," Eleanor stated.

Diana looked at the dark blue jumpsuit. It was different from the one worn by the other operatives. Eleanor had found herself one to get out of her own formal attire.

The two of them got re-dressed and then regrouped at the table.

"We have plenty of space in the rear of the warehouse for a makeshift firing range, ma'am," one of the operatives said in an Australian accent.

"It will have to do," Agent Black replied. "Take the girl out to show her the ropes in guerilla tactics for me, Sergeant Mendez."

"Yes, ma'am," the other male operative replied in an American accent.

The Australian operative had short blonde hair and tanned skin, while the other had lighter olive-style skin and blackish-brown hair. He looked to be Hispanic, while the other appeared to be of Anglo descent like Diana and Eleanor – outside of the tan. The Hispanic operative had a chiseled jaw – he was taller than the other operative who was about five-feet and eleven-inches whereas the other was six-feet and two-inches tall. Agent Black was about an inch taller than Diana if not the same height. The Hispanic operative was clean-shaven whereas the other was unshaven.

"Alright, kid. Take a rifle and let's go," Sergeant Mendez said to Diana.

"Sure thing," Diana replied, taking an assault rifle on the ground and a few clips.

The Hispanic operative, Sergeant Mendez, took the rifle on the table and a backpack. He then led Diana down an aisle. Diana turned around and looked at Agent Black as she remained with Lieutenant Carse. The sergeant led Diana outside where the sun had started to set, leaving an orange hue down on the ground alongside a warmth in the humid desert air.

Sergeant Mendez led Diana out a couple of stretches before stopping close to the surrounding perimeter of the compound and turning to her. Diana paid close attention to the sergeant as he looked at her.

"At ease," the sergeant said. "This isn't the military. Given the circumstances, we're going to have to cut the discipline portion and get straight to it. Have you ever fired a weapon like this before?"

"N-never an assault rifle like this," Diana confessed. "Only a pistol."

"I'm not surprised because you're holding it wrong. Keep your hand away from that muzzle and get your finger off the trigger. Move your hand back a bit and twist your other hand so that you've got a finger above the trigger, but not on the trigger. The rest of your hand should be providing support to keep the gun up so that you can point forwards."

Diana readjusted her technique. Her heart was beating steadily, but quickly as she held the rifle in her hands. She was intimidated at the size of the weapon and its weight.

"Now, show me your firing stance," the sergeant asked.

Diana leaned forward and pointed the weapon forward. She rested the butt of the gun against her shoulder and maintained her hands at the previous position.

"Now, look down your scope and try to get the cacti in the distance with the hole atop of the gun – those are your iron sights."

"Right," Diana replied, peaking one eye through. "I've got the cacti in my sights."

Diana pressed her finger down on the trigger and felt her cheeks flush as nothing came through. She pressed down several more times before bringing the weapon down and realizing that she had forgotten to load the weapon with a clip.

"Yeah, that's what I thought," Mendez replied, looking at her with a condescending frown. "It's one thing to see an enemy and another to be ready to fire. You've got to load the gun and ready it, but even before that, you've got to check your safety. Take a magazine and bring it into the slot underneath the gun."

Diana took a magazine and fiddled with it before feeling it slide in.

"Now that you've got the magazine in, cock it and you'll be ready for action. Like this."

Sergeant Mendez put a magazine into his own rifle, cocked it with a trigger on the side of the gun and then rested. He looked over to Diana to do the same. Diana cocked the gun and then brought herself into a readied stance. She then looked forward through the scope of the gun.

"Good, now fire at the three closest cacti behind the fence."

Diana lined the first one up and opened fire. The kick of the rifle from the volume of the bullets being sprayed caused the muzzle to tip up, especially with her weak grip. Diana held through and shifted to look down at the other plant in the distance. She opened fire at them before stopping to rest the gun, pointed it downwards.

"Good, now we're getting somewhere."

"Is that all there is to it? What else could you possibly have me learn?" Diana asked.

"Kid, we're just getting started. There's a lot more to learn."

. .

By midnight, the rear of the warehouse had been converted into an obstacle course, incorporating parts of the actual warehouse with it to utilize all they had.

Diana stepped forward at the start line with a pistol drawn in both hands. She looked down and waited for the sound of the whistle that let her move forward. At its sound, Diana rushed forward and knelt down, opening fire at the crash dummies tied to various props before her. Diana shot at the dummy behind the jeep and then she fired at the one behind a series of crates. Once the targets were down, Diana stood up and rushed around a large truck that was parked and blocked the rest of the outside portion of the course.

Once she came around, Diana knelt down again and opened fire at the target behind the truck, a knocked over desk, and the next target next to her behind a forklift. She then focused ahead at the two dummies underneath the water tower, but avoided the one dressed in a blue jumpsuit. However, she did shoot the naked one next to it instead.

Afterwards, Diana stood back up again and rushed around the water tower since her path to the door into the warehouse had been artificially blocked by a line in the concrete. She quickly sprinted around, stopping at the entrance where two more dummies were stood guard before turning her attention to the ones on the roof. Her bullets ripped through each one, letting her continue as soon as she got conformation to herself that she hit them.

Diana ran up the door of the warehouse and with a quick, but careful hand, she opened it, taking a moment before letting herself in. She rushed forward, opening fire at the dummy behind a knocked over table in the first aisle before dropping down behind some empty oil drums to use as her own cover.

The dummies had different locations each turn of taking the obstacle course to train Diana's reflexes. Mendez had changed some of them and others he kept to trick Diana as she was forced to focus on some other exercises while he set up. Diana focused on the dummies ahead. One in front of the cover in a jumpsuit and other behind the cover leading into the final aisle that was naked. She ignored this target in favor of the other one exposed, taped to some cargo underneath the second shelf before moving herself into the second aisle to get into cover and a clear shot at the dummy in the end of the warehouse.

Diana shot it and looked at the two targets in the aisle she had to get through to get to the end. She fired at both of them and then proceeded forward as fast as she could to beat her former time record.

Suddenly, a dummy dropped down in the middle of the aisle, startling Diana to draw her combat knife at the prop and slice it in the middle. She withdrew the knife and then continued to the end.

"On the catwalk!" Mendez shouted, causing Diana to pause and look up.

Diana quickly opened fire at the two dummies on the catwalk above the garage door of the warehouse, taking them out for him to move to the end where one last dummy sat in the chair at a table. Diana took her last shot and then crossed the finish line where Mendez waited for her.

"Not bad, kid."

"I didn't miss any," Diana reported to him as she panted.

"I'll decide on that," Mendez replied, standing up from his chair. "Go meet up with Agent Black and Lieutenant Carse in the other warehouse while I go check. You've done good today. We've got lots more to cover tomorrow morning."

"Yes, sir," Diana replied, nodding to him before leaving.

Diana took a deep sigh as soon as they parted. She left behind her equipment and then ran over to the next warehouse. Her body trembled and looked as though she would collapse at any moment.

Eleanor and Carse were in the same position they were last in about two hours ago. Each of them were hunched over a table, plotting. The warehouse smelt of cigarette smoke and sure enough, Eleanor was smoking. She straightened up as she noticed Diana come in, causing the lieutenant to turn around and look at her.

"Sergeant Mendez dismissed me," Diana stated.

"Yes, it's time you got some rest. We've got more for you to learn at dawn," she said, tapping her cigarette into an ash tray. "Lieutenant Carse and I are still putting together a plan. We'll go over the details with you in the morning."

"Right," Diana replied, eyeing her cigarette with a focused eye.

Agent Black noticed this attention and picked up her box of smokes, presenting them to Diana who stood across the warehouse from her.

"Interested in one?" she asked.

"I don't smoke," Diana replied.

"Hm," she responded, "that's not what your profile says, Ms. Cambridge."

Diana looked at her intently before taking a step back and turning to leave. She placed any remaining equipment with her at a table nearby before leaving quietly.

"Goodnight, Ms. Cambridge," Eleanor said.

Diana looked over to her and nodded. She then left into the humid night that laid around the compound. She walked across the street and down the side of the road. The night was quiet, the crickets were chirping, and there was a light wind in the air passing through. Her stomach grumbled, but she was too tired to eat and simply aimed for the barracks.

From the warehouse, Diana walked to the center of the road and turned down along a pathway that led to the barracks she had to sleep in. Diana made her way down half of the path before she came to a bench to take a seat. She looked around and crossed her arms. She then decided to lay back as she closed her eyes. She listened to the ambience around her – the howl of a coyote in the distance, the orchestra of insects nearby, and the wind in the background.

Suddenly, the sound of a jeep approaching and stopping nearby also caught her attention. Diana opened her eyes and looked over to see who had arrived. It was Tristan with his own team. Dr. Brown led them towards a barrack that he had unlocked for them. He then allowed them in. Tristan took notice of Diana sitting down nearby and diverted from the crew to walk over to her.

"Training hard, I see," Tristan said as he got close.

"Don't even talk to me," she replied, looking up to the sky as she laid back again.

"Sorry?"

"I just got off," Diana clarified. "I'm dead tired and have to get up in the next six hours for more."

"Oh…" Tristan replied, sitting down next to her.

"It's okay. I asked for this, I guess. I didn't realize that it would be this tough. God knows how sore I'm going to be in the morning."

"We're doing what we can," Tristan said, putting a hand over Diana's.

Diana tilted her head back up immediately to look over to Tristan. He was dressed in his own jumpsuit, but his had the Cabernet Space logo on the right breast.

"I'm not happy about you volunteering yourself to go into that base," Tristan stated, "but I'm also proud of you because few people could do what you're going to do."

"What I'm doing? I'm not doing much compared to you."

"Well, all I did today was sit in a classroom," Tristan explained, sighing. "It's not like being at school though."

"Because there'll be no tests?"

"No," Tristan replied, "being in that ship will be our test and if I make even one mistake, then that could mean the end of myself, the mission, all my crewmates – and the rest of the world. I realized that as we went on and on about a bunch of technicalities."

"You just made me more scared for you," Diana said with a worried expression.

"Sorry."

"You're smart. Just remember that you can't afford to mess up," Diana remarked, bringing a hand to Tristan's cheek. "You've got me."

"I know," Tristan nodded. "You're my motivation to go up and back down in one-piece. I won't let you down. I won't let you…"

"Stop."

"You don't even know what I was going to say."

"I do. You don't have to repeat it to me," Diana said, noticing Tristan's eyes wander behind Diana.

Tristan let go of Diana's hand and used his other to bring Diana's down from his cheek.

"Moira incoming," Tristan explained.

Diana turned and saw her best friend coming down the path on her own. She hadn't noticed them yet as she walked with her eyes on the ground, pacing herself as she reached the barracks.

"How's the codebreaking going?" Diana asked as she came near.

Moira took a deep sigh and looked over to them.

"Not good. I don't think we've made much progress today."

"Oh…" Diana replied.

"Dr. Lambert sent me to get some sleep. She said she was going to do the same and let the alien with the angelic voice takeover once she's become familiar with our codes. Do these… things… sleep?"

Diana shrugged.

"I haven't seen it eat," Diana added. "I don't even know if they're real."

"They're so skinny," Tristan remarked. "I mean, the diameter of their limbs are childlike. It's insane."

"Anyways, are you okay?" Diana asked Moira.

'Not really. I mean, I'm doing what I can to help, but we're not making progress which has me a bit down."

"Well, you've practically been kidnapped to join us. Charles said he was going to let you call your parents. Did you talk to your dad?" Diana questioned.

"Yeah, Charles visited us about an hour ago and let me talk to him. I told him I'm having a sleepover with you, and he believed me…"

"Right."

Tristan yawned and stood up before saying," Well, we should get some sleep. We've probably all got to get up early, so I'm going to bed."

"Good idea,' Diana sighed. "Let's go."

Act 5, Scene 3

"Merrick, it's time to go," Captain Poulsson said.

Tristan opened his eyes, leaning forward as he woke up with a lingering fatigue. He saw the captain ahead of him as he wiped his eyes with his arm. Captain Poulsson was dressed in his jumpsuit and leaning against the bunkbed opposite of Tristan's.

"I didn't oversleep, did I?" Tristan questioned.

"No, but if you don't hurry, you'll miss breakfast and be late. Get moving," Poulsson said, pushing himself from where he stood and turning to leave. "I'll give you ten minutes to get ready."

Tristan nodded and got out of bed. He grabbed his boots and went to the back of the barracks where the washroom was. He took a quick shower and re-dressed himself in his jumpsuit before leaving to meet the other astronaut outside.

It was about seven o'clock in the morning when Tristan left the barracks to join the others in the small dining hall nearby. The option for food was limited with the limited staff available. After breakfast, all three of them were joined by Dr. Brown who took them to the astronaut training facility at the opposite end of the tarmac from the shuttle hangar. They had their first round of lessons in a classroom for the first two hours, and then by mid-morning, they were brought to what Dr. Brown called, 'the neutral buoyancy laboratory.'

"Isn't it a sight to see?" the doctor questioned as the astronauts and him stood outside in the hall, looking through a window into the large room.

Tristan looked through into the large room that stretched for about three-hundred and sixty feet from the side they were at. In the middle was a large pool that was about four times the length of a standard Olympic-sized swimming pool. Inside the pool were a series of strange metallic structures littered through like an underwater playground. Various mechanisms were seen around the pool as well.

"Anyways, enough ogling," Dr. Brown said, leading the team forward down the hall. "We must get you fitted into the right equipment before you dive with our safety team. I talked with Mr. Cabernet who approved additional staffing this morning so that I could properly train you."

Dr. Brown led the team into the laboratory where three models of the spacesuit they were to wear were attached to three separate cranes. The suits almost resembled the traditional white space suits, but they were dark grey and slightly slimmer. They were still bulky and had chords strapped to the back, connecting into a separate machine for the purpose of the simulation.

"These are your extreme environment suits, and they will protect you from radiation and the pressure of space," Dr. Brown said. "Of course, these are models of the ones you'll actually be wearing. The real ones will be lighter and more comfortable. Unlike the suits worn by the public-sector, these are far more advanced, but still fragile as they've yet to be finished. You can tell by some exposed wires at the front."

Tristan saw the wiring. It was a flat thin group of wires that extended from the pelvis area and tied around to go up into the suit from the spine. The biggest difference between this suit and the standard government-issued suits was the helmet. It wasn't round, but instead oval, connecting with the top-piece of the suit through a hood that blended together. The backpiece was missing too.

Two assistants came around with a type of thin garment with tubs from the sides underneath the arm pits.

"For this exercise, you won't be wearing your jumpsuits underneath the extreme environment suits, but instead these

Liquid Cooling Garments, or LCG. They'll regulate your body temperature and make sure you don't overheat," Dr. Brown explained. "I'll let you get changed into them before we fit the trial space suits."

Tristan took one of the white garments into his hand and followed the rest of the crew with getting undressed. Once he was re-dressed, he felt he coldness of the liquid as soon as the woman connected his suit with a small device that went around him through the help of a belt. In a brief second, Tristan felt cold from the sweat he was in due to his anxiety.

"This suit connects with our computers to give us feedback on your biometric data," Dr. Brown explained. "That way, we can record and override the system in case of malfunction. Now though, let's get you three suited up for the simulation.

It took longer than expected, but with the help of the support staff, Tristan got the boots and leg pieces together before he was helped to the platform that would be dropped down into the water. Dr. Brown handed Tristan a headset device. It was silver in color and made of chrome. It had a single headphone on the right-end with a headband that twisted over and around the back and front. Attached from the headband was a microphone going down and an antenna going up. Tristan put it on and adjusted the size so that it wasn't too tight. He then ducked down and brought his body up through the suit, fitting his arms into each appropriate space before his head went into the helmet.

Tristan looked through the glass and everybody around him as they helped finish putting the torso-piece together with the leg-piece. Each piece felt immense from the lead linings used to simulate pressure in the suit.

"Are you okay, Mr. Merrick?" Dr. Brown asked him.

"Yeah, I'm good," Tristan replied, hearing his own voice echo from within his suit.

"Alright, let's raise the crane and get you into the water."

Tristan staggered as he felt the platform move, raising him with his torso still attached to the crane. Scuba divers dropped into the tank as he was raised up and then dipped into the pool with the others. He breathed slowly as he found himself submerged, feeling the other lining of the suit press at his skin, causing the adapted suit to respond and counteract the pressure.

Bubbles rose above him, and suddenly, he felt the back portion of the suit release from the crane, allowing him to hover where he stood in zero buoyancy. The scuba divers made their approach to him.

"All units, this is a radio check. How copy, over?" Dr. Brown projected from the surface.

"Copy," Captain Poulsson replied.

"Copy," Sergeant Zajaczkowski added.

"Copy," Tristan repeated as the scuba divers helped him move forward.

"Alright, Alpha Team, we're bringing you to the first course as discussed in the briefing. To recap, the Lindworm will bring you to the target location where you will exit and proceed with your classified assignment."

Tristan drifted with them, feeling no resistance from the water to cause him to float either up or down. Instead, he simply moved with the divers as they brought him towards one of the structures deep under the pool.

The water was perfectly clear, giving Tristan impeccable visibility to all around him. The various metallic structures, one of which mimicked a space shutter exterior, made the entire underwater space look like an underwater lost city.

The assistants brought Tristan and the other astronauts to the replica of the space shutter. It was strange-looking with half of the dorsal side completely missing, leaving behind a sort of curved trench exposed cockpit. Tristan and the crew were brought down to touch their feet at the surface.

"Proceed to the airlock and we can begin the simulation," Dr. Brown ordered.

Tristan followed either Captain Poulsson or Sergeant Zajaczkowski who landed ahead of him in the pit. He tried to walk forward but couldn't. Although they were in a pool, they were still on Earth and certain restrictions were placed on the suit to prevent Tristan from swimming his way around.

The three of them were helped forward for the remaining distance, into the hollow tube that went into the cockpit of the model shuttle before the doors of the tube closed to simulate the airlock. The roof of the tube and cockpit were displaced to allow for the umbilical cords providing air into the suits, protruding from the back like tales to move around.

"Alright, bring Mr. Merrick forward first," Dr. Brown said over the radio.

"Copy," Poulsson replied.

The first door of the airlock opened. Tristan grabbed hold of a handle near the door and guided himself trough. He gently crashed into the other door and heard the opposite shut on its own. There were handles along the bottom of the airlock to resemble rungs of a ladder. Tristan looked at them, but instead brought his fingers to the edge of the airlock as the doors opened, and he pushed himself out with both hands. He then took hold of some rungs in the center floor of the pit to stop himself from floating to the opposite end.

"Are you okay, Mr. Merrick?" Dr. Brown asked.

"I'm fine," Tristan replied, taking a deep breath. "I'm just getting used to this."

The crew ran through the rest of the simulation where they were to leave the spaceship and touch down on the floor of the pool, which was simulating the surface of the capital ship they were to land on. They went through the entire process several times before having themselves run exercises in certain components of the space shuttle in case they were to breakdown.

By mid-noon, scuba divers were helping Tristan back to the crane so that he could be brought out. Suddenly, the gloves of Tristan's suit ruptured their connection from the torso-piece, causing Tristan to jump in fright and feel the pressure of his suit drift out of him while his hands tried to float upwards.

"What's happening?" Tristan questioned.

"Relax, I only want to explain the event of a puncture to you," Dr. Brown replied. "The most important tip is to remain calm. Watch."

Tristan watched as his oxygen left his suit with bubbles of air rising as the pressure of the suit shrank, dragging an immense weight onto Tristan's shoulder. Eventually, the flow stopped. He took a deep breath and then moved his hands around before he was brought out of the water finally.

"Did I run out of oxygen?" Tristan asked.

"No, the suit regulated itself and cut-off connections to your hand to prevent further loss of oxygen. In the unlikely event of a tear, this is what will happen when you are in space."

"Okay…" Tristan replied.

The crane brought Tristan out of the water and set him down. Staff began to unlatch every part of the suit before removing the torso.

Tristan took another sigh as stood in his LCG, completely drive. He began to remove the top-piece of the garment, rolling it down his torso to leave his torso exposed before being interrupted by Dr. Brown as he came over.

"Good work," Mr. Merrick. How does the transition from the weightlessness to weight feel?"

"It's strange…" Tristan answered, "but I'm glad to be able to use my legs again."

"Yes, I remember when I returned to the Earth after being on the I.S.S. for six months. It was a transition I will never forget," Dr. Brown reminisced, taking a deep sigh.

"You were on the international space station?" Tristan questioned. "Why aren't you coming with us instead?"

"I cannot. I have lost my health and am too old. That's why I work with Cabernet Space as an engineer and consultant instead of being an astronaut."

"Right…" Tristan replied.

"You did well, Mr. Merrick. You're dismissed for the next hour. Meet me at the entrance of this building then. Until then, have your lunch and relax," Dr. Brown said.

"Thank you," Tristan replied, nodding to him.

Dr. Brown bowed his head before leaving to talk to the other astronauts. Tristan located his jumpsuit and boots and went over to grab them before he left the pool to get changed in the changing rooms.

• •

"I don't know how many more days I have to train you three, but the longer we have, the deeper and better understanding you will have in what usually takes two years to master," Dr. Brown explained as he drove down the tarmac later at midnight.

"You must understand that we cannot export this task to anybody else," Captain Poulsson replied.

"Yes, I know," Dr. Brown said, nodding. "Mr. Cabernet explained to me in detail yesterday all of it. We've taken a task that even NASA or the ESA would struggle with in this time limit. I only hope for more time than anything else… I'm confident in you three, and I suppose you will have ground support to guide you in what you're unfamiliar with, but there's a reason that these missions take an arduous amount of time to plan – it is so that the rarest of scenarios where something might go wrong are understood and that you're prepared to handle them. My worst nightmare would be for you to go up there and lose connection with us. We are doing the best we can, and I appreciate your understanding in that."

"Goodnight, doctor," Poulsson replied, opening the door as they stopped.

"Goodnight, you three. I'll be back tomorrow morning."

"Goodnight," Tristan confirmed, opening the door to step out.

Tristan made his way down the path behind the other two as they chatted between each other, but instead of going inside with Tristan, they split paths from him and joined up with the other two agents that defected and were part of Diana's team. Tristan didn't make much of it and instead went inside. He stopped underneath the beam of the door to notice a single light on at a bunkbed towards the middle-right. Tristan tilted his head down to see who it was, giving a light smile to realize that it was Diana.

Diana had her back against her bunk, head tilted down and was deep asleep. Tristan quietly walked forward and turned down the space between his and her bunk to get a better look. A magazine was over her torso, pressed down by her hand. She was still in her jumpsuit and her hair was messy and unkempt. She had one leg with her boot still in, stretched over the bed while the other was kept on the ground.

"Hey," Tristan quietly said, bringing a hand over Diana's to gently wake her.

"Hmm?" Diana replied, opening her eyes to look at Tristan. "Oh, it's you. Is it morning already?"

"No, it's just past midnight. You fell asleep still dressed."

"Oh," Diana replied, blinking hard as she regained consciousness. "How did it go? The training? Did you enjoy zero gravity?"

"It's not called 'zero gravity,'" Tristan replied, sitting down at his own bunk. "It's called weightlessness, and it was really weird and slightly unpleasant."

"Oh."

"Any ways, after that, they took me for a ride in a jet before they moved me for a parabolic flight so I could feel weightlessness again, but without the suit."

"Did you puke?"

Tristan shook his head before saying," I'm clear for the launch. Any idea when we're going?"

"Nope," Diana replied. "Could be tomorrow – it could be next week or next month. I spoke to Moira around noon and she said that they still haven't been able to crack the security system."

"Jeez, is it that bad?" Tristan asked as Diana adjusted herself to sit up.

"Well, I haven't heard otherwise, so I assume it is."

"Have you talked to Charles? I haven't seen him since we got here. I hope he isn't wearing himself out too much."

Diana shook his head in rejection as she looked to the side. Tristan leaned forward and took Diana's hand, causing her to look back at him.

"How was your day?" Tristan asked.

"I'm sore and tried," she replied.

"Well, that makes both of us."

"The most interesting thing we did today was try out this new suit that Charles managed to put together with the help of Mika. It's a stealth camouflage suit that can make us invisible."

"Invisible, or blobs of distorted space?" Tristan asked.

"Invisible," Diana replied. "According to your friend, Mika, I could see him when he cloaks himself because I'm young. Similar to how young people can hear certain frequencies that adults can't, the camouflage works the same. It's why Charles and Judith couldn't see the alien when I first brought her to Cabernet Laboratories."

"Her? Is that thing even a girl?"

"Is Mika a dude? I'm just assuming," Diana replied, shrugging. "It's what they've been referring themselves as. Besides, her voice is different from the others – it's angelic and smooth, like a woman's. His voice is deeper and coarse, like a man's. We've been taking to referring her as Madonna recently because she needed a name – even if it's just a codename."

"Madonna..." Tristan repeated. "Interesting choice... it's not like those voices are their real voices. They're nothing but artificial voices – these beings don't even have vocal cords."

Diana shrugged, closing her eyes for a moment before opening them to look ahead to him. She tilted her head and looked at Tristan.

"I'm really, really tired. I also miss being in my bed with you."

"Me too, Diana," Tristan replied. "Me too..."

Tristan gave a sigh.

"Why do we even have to sleep? I barely slept at all last night because I'm anxious about what's to come."

"If we didn't ever sleep, we would never have a reason to cuddle at night."

"I was being rhetorical. I know why we have to sleep. It's to recharge ourselves, our brains, our bodies. It's to let our meninges recycle itself and filter all the toxins of our strained cells."

"Well, there you go being a know-it-all smart ass," Diana replied.

Tristan smiled at her and let go of Diana's hand.

"You haven't kissed me for a while," Tristan said, looking at Diana.

"I didn't think you'd keep track of something like that," Diana replied, turning his head up.

"Huh?" Tristan replied, surprised by his answer. "Of course I'd keep track."

Diana tilted her head down and looked towards the doorway.

"There's no privacy in a place like this – not that we're together during the day. A part of me wishes this never happened and another wants it to be over," Diana said. "I'd kiss you right now too, but I have a gut feeling that any second now, Moira is going to come through that door to force us apart."

"Life might never be the same after all of this. I mean, we're on the edge of a total global war that could end the human species," Tristan said. "We might be training with exception that we'll be going up, but it might come to war first, or Moira and them might learn that the life in that vessel was killed, and then we'll have been too late. Nothing is directional here, Diana. It's the end of days."

"Right… thanks for that depressing summary of the situation."

"Sorry, I'm just… I'm really tired and it was bringing me down keeping all that in my head."

Diana gave an understanding look. Tristan brought his hands to his face. He then took them away, stood up and walked over to Diana's bunk. He sat down at her feet and started to untie her boots before removing them. He then helped Diana into bed before bringing a hand to her cheek.

"Get some sleep, okay?" Tristan said, cutting their midnight conversation short. "I love you."

Diana had already fallen asleep before the last words came out. Tristan kissed her goodnight before straightening up as he faced his own bunk.

A creak of wood from the doorway spooked him, causing him to turn and face Moira as she entered the barracks.

"Oh, it's you," Tristan whispered.

"Yeah, it's me," Moira replied, walking over to him.

"How's the hacking going?"

"It's going... still no progress..." she replied with a sigh, climbing up the bunk over Diana's after removing her boots.

"Right, well, I'll let you catch some sleep then. I'm beat."

"Same," she replied from over her bunk.

"Goodnight," Tristan said, looking over to her with a slight shyness as she got into bed.

"Night," she replied.

Moira turned her back to him, letting Tristan take a deep breath before looking to Diana. He turned off the light between them and got into bed. He then closed his eyes, falling asleep instantly.

Act 5, Scene 4

Charlemagne rode the elevator of the main building up to the third-floor. The doors of the lift opened, revealing the short grey hallway going to another set of silver doors that mimicked the elevator doors. The door had a security panel next to it and led into a dark, short corridor with a glass window next to it looking into a server room. The hallway came to another set of thick doors and security panel, which he went to. The security panel light turned green after Charlemagne pressed his hand on the screen. The door then slid open for him to enter the operations center of Cabernet Space.

An aisle from the door led down to three large monitors on the farthest wall. Four rows of interconnected desks ran on each side with computers littered in a chain. The room was dark and dim lights were turned on at various stations and pouring through computer monitors left on.

Madonna stood next to Charlemagne from where he entered. She looked at him before looking back at the screen ahead. One projected a map of the entire globe, and the other two different screens from the computers within. In the row opposite from where the alien stood, stood Judith holding herself by her arms against a railing. In the row in front of her sat Eleanor Black at a computer.

Charlemagne walked over to stand next to Judith.

"Has any progress been met?" Charlemagne asked.

"None," Judith replied. "It's more difficult than we thought. How about you? How has progress come on the spaceship?"

"The Lindworm is coming along with Barry's help. I haven't done much to avoid getting in the way. I've been working on other miscellaneous tasks around the base."

"Ah, I heard about the tactical suits you made yesterday," Judith replied. "I must say, I'm envious."

"I barely did much. It was our friend, the one that's being called 'Mika' that gave us their secrets into stealth camouflage. My God, it was such a simple method that we've been blind to as well. We were only able to produce two suits, and I'm hoping that one goes to Diana to keep her out of danger."

"You're insane to let her go," Judith whispered.

"I have no choice," he whispered back. "Besides, you heard of what could happen if she doesn't help. Millions of children more could lose their lives if a war were to break out."

Charlemagne brought his hands to his eyes, placing his thumb and index fingers on his temples respectively.

"Get some rest, Charles. How long have you been awake?"

"Not as long as you."

"I've been fine here. You must be more exhausted leading us through this. Don't let the stress get to you," she added, putting a hand on Charles.

Charlemagne quickly looked over to her as she lent a smile to him. He maintained a tired and exhausted expression with strained eyes. Judith brought her hand up and placed it on his cheek. She lowered her own smile to focus on Charlemagne a bit more seriously. She then leaned in.

"She's done it!" Eleanor loudly remarked. "That girl has really done it!"

The two adults retracted, turning their gaze from each other and down to Agent Black's computer.

"What is it?" Charlemagne asked.

"Come and see for yourself," she replied.

Charlemagne and Judith came around and stood behind Agent Black as she showed them her screen. It was black with lines of code running from the top to the bottom in small lines.

"I couldn't help but focus on what Ms. Macmillan had done up to this point after letting her go and get some rest. She told me that could infiltrate the Global Defense Project's network undetected but required an entrance to get in so-to-speak. I took what she had done and put it through an entrance, and now, I believe we're in."

"What? Into the entire system?" Charlemagne asked.

"Exactly, without detection, just as I had asked her to do this time."

"Amazing," Judith replied. "All on her own."

"From here, I can access the personal log-in of our chief of research, see what he's been doing, and find out what's happened to that rock," Eleanor explained, navigating herself through the system files.

"How long will that take?" Judith questioned.

"I've found it."

"Well?" Charlemagne asked.

"I worked with this organization – I'm familiar with its system. It was a part of the greater system. I have emails sent from today to Director Selebi," Eleanor said.

"What have they done?" Charlemagne asked, trying to read them himself.

Agent Black scrolled through and read email to email. She then closed the last and opened the next.

"It appears that they're having some difficulties finding a material that is strong enough to even dent the outer shell. All the preliminary examinations have been finished, however," she explained.

"So, it's still in one-piece then?" Charlemagne replied.

"For now," Eleanor said, opening the previous document. "A report from today says that they've overcome this obstacle and are waiting for engineers to put together a drill powerful enough to let them cut through."

"Well, that was quick. How long will it take for them to put that together?" Judith asked.

"Hm…" she replied, scrolling through and reading. "Engineering is working as fast as they can, and it could be ready as soon as later today."

"Today? That would put…" Charlemagne paused for a moment as he looked to the side and sighed.

"A vivisection of the vessel is scheduled in the next twenty-four hours or so," Eleanor announced. "We have that much time to prepare."

Charlemagne and Judith looked at each other.

"Are you and your crew ready to assault the base?" Charlemagne asked, looking down to Eleanor.

"My crew is. We'll buy you some time to prepare the others by going in and extracting the cargo. Perhaps we won't need to go into space at all if we can delay this."

"I would advise against that," Madonna replied from behind.

The three of them turned to her.

"Should you fail, and the life in that vessel be destroyed, they will be notified immediately and strike. All that keeps peace between our worlds is the life in that vessel and in me. I would advise that you proceed with the mission as originally planned."

"What is it about you that negates war?" Eleanor asked with suspicion.

"I am the only one that can communicate with the command center," the alien answered. "My partner cannot. It is my rank that allows me to and not him."

"I see," Eleanor answered.

"We're not ready though," Judith said. "Charles said it himself. The ship is not ready and our astronauts have barely trained."

"We'll launch in twenty-four hours. I'll call in more support and we'll get the spacecraft moved and readied for launch," Charlemagne remarked.

"I thought it wasn't ready," Judith replied, slightly annoyed.

"No, it isn't, but we have no choice. The best I can do is accelerate development and launch in whatever shape it is in – granted that it is in a shape to launch. It does have enough integrity to fly upwards, but don't expect a ride back."

"I will ensure transport from my people aboard one of our own vessels," Madonna replied.

"Thank you," Charlemagne said, nodding before looking down to Eleanor as she stood up.

"We have twenty-four hours left. Let's not waste them."

"I'll look through these files and put together a method for your team to enter the base with ease – to bypass any security systems and give you a skeleton key in," Judith said, walking over to sit down at the desk.

"Very well then," Eleanor replied.

Act 5, Scene 5

"Thanks to the work of Dr. Lambert and Ms. Macmillan, we've managed to hack our way into the exposed servers of the Global Defense Project and learn that our Primary Target is scheduled for termination at approximately 0400 hours," Agent Black explained at the front of the operations center.

The room was darker than usual with the other computers and lamps off, leaving only the three front screens on. Everybody was in the room, listening and watching as they were briefed on the operation. The defected operatives stood at the back on the right-side, while the four engineers on the opposite-end. At the front, Dr. Brown, Charlemagne, Judith and Barry sat together on a left side row of desks, close to the aisle. Diana and Tristan sat with Moira in the desks in front of the soldiers, again, closer to the aisle. Moira was at her computer, controlling the projections of the briefing that went on the screens in the front. The aliens stood together in front of the door of the center.

"According to our extraterrestrial friends, the moment the Primary Target is aborted, the orbiting fleet will be notified and given clearance to assault the Earth. Based on some assumptions and research done in my time with the G.D.P., the aliens will be sure to assault major and highly densely populated areas, such as Harlech, Los Angeles, Chicago, New York, London, Paris, New Delhi, and Beijing..."

"Jesus..." an operative whispered from behind the kids.

"... I can only imagine the weaponry this civilization possesses, and so, we must be as cautious as possible. Bravo Team, led by me, will be leaving as soon as possible from here and travelling up north to the location of the G.D.P. headquarters in the Tongass National Forest in southern Alaska."

The middle screen showed satellite imagery of the forest with no traces of the secret headquarters in the land.

"There are only two ways to get into the G.D.P. HQ. The first is through a cavern that leads to the elevator shaft, and the other is the most obvious method – the hangar doors going into the hangar. At sunset, we will give an anonymous tip of alien activity on the opposite-side of the world. The G.D.P. will have no choice but to scramble their last V-TOL and some of their troops. Exposed, we will have enough time for us to strike and come back. At 0100 hours, Bravo Team will leave and travel north. Utilizing the security clearance codes accessed by our research team, we will override the hangar doors and land in the main hangar. From there, no doubt, we will be forced to confront the security forces where I will be forced to explain my sudden disappearance as well as the disappearance of Mr. Cabernet. I will explain that I used Mr. Cabernet as a means of locating an E.T. With Ms. Cambridge and Sergeant Mendez utilizing stealth camouflage and Ms. Macmillan remaining aboard the V-TOL, we will escort Mika with Lieutenant Carse. Of course, additional troops will come to our side. Once we are in a secured location, Ms. Cambridge and Sergeant Mendez will reveal themselves at a vantage point and force our escort to lower their weapons. By this method, we will have gained access into the base. From the containment cells, Bravo Team will travel back up and through the rest of the headquarters to get to the director's office and server room. From here, I will be able to arrest the director and get into contact with the Committee. Once done, I will be in full control of the base's activities, including scientific research. I will have our scientists cease their experimentations on the Primary Target immediately before 0400 hours. We will then wait with confirmation from Charlemagne about the status of Bravo Team from here and meet them on the surface. Charles?"

"Thank you," Charlemagne replied, standing up to take over.

The projection on screen changed to footage of the Lindworm in position at the landing pad and ready to launch.

"At 2300 hours, two hours before Bravo Team leave," Charlemagne said. "Alpha Team will launch with the Lindworm at a speed of nearly 30,000 kilometers per hour. From there, the booster rockets will aid in the ascent until about 70,000 meters above sea level, which is when the external tanks and boosters will detach. Their targeted trajectory will be the Kennte River, which is where staff will be waiting nearby to recover the pieces. The rocket will reach a maximum of about 256,000 kilometers per hour with the help of a fusion engine, letting Alpha Team arrive at their computer-marked destination on the capital ship around the same time that Bravo Team leaves from Kennte to go to Alaska. Alpha Team's task is simple – to gain access into the capital ship and escort our VIP, codename 'Madonna,' to her destination. From there, Madonna will report to her superiors about their acquisition of the vessel. She will then provide transport for Alpha Team to return to Earth and meet Bravo Team and Charlie Team outside of the G.D.P. headquarters."

The screen changed once more to the logo of Cabernet Space before Charlemagne could continue.

"Charlie Team, led by me, will remain in this room and act as mission control for both teams. We will be available for support and tactical analysis. Joining me will be both Dr. Lamberts, Dr. Brown and our engineers. We will act as a medium between both teams, and when each team has completed their missions, they will be letting us know."

"I know some of us aren't as conditioned as we should be for this mission, and I know that all of us are equally nervous, but we're all that stands in the way between life and death for this world of ours," Eleanor said. "We are about to embark upon one of the most dangerous undertakings of human history, and nobody except those of which are in this room will know of it. There will be no medals. There will be no glory. There will be no praise. There will only be defeat or victory. None of us should want anything more than total victory. We are here because we understand what is most important – to defend the innocent, because that is who we are. We are Guardians of this Earth. Good luck and let us beseech the blessing of Almighty God upon this great and noble undertaking."

"Godspeed," Charlemagne added.

Act 6, Scene 1

"Are you ready, kid?" Captain Poulsson questioned Tristan.

Tristan looked away from himself in the mirror and over to Poulsson. He nodded.

"Let's go then."

Tristan looked back at himself and examined the Advanced Crew Escape (ACE) suit he was given to wear for the launch. It was different to the Extravehicular Activities (EVA) suit from earlier. The dark orange material on the outside was a synthetic fire-retardant material commonly used by firefighters. It had with it a backpack and a small tube that ran down all the way along Tristan's left thigh and into his suit to adjust pressure with oxygen. It was off at the moment because he still hadn't put on his helmet and was sitting on a bench.

An orange harness blended into the suit and he had various pockets: two at his thighs, lower legs, and another two on his breast. His gloves were orange and they had black cuffs at the wrist where the two-pieces met. The suit came down to his modified paratrooper black boots and wrapped tightly around his ankles.

Tristan took a step back and retrieved his helmet, looking into his reflection in the black tint before leaving. Underneath his suit, he wore his dark blue jumpsuit with a thermal one-piece to keep him warm. He wore a similar headset to the one given to him during the various training missions: the headset with one earpiece and headband that extended around and over his head to secure its placement.

The building was deserted. Tristan followed Captain Poulsson outside to where Dr. Brown was waiting for them with a nervous and worried expression. He was with Sergeant Zajaczkowski.

"Let me just take a look," Dr. Brown said, going to Captain Poulsson to make sure his suit was properly adjusted.

Dr. Brown then went to Tristan. He tightened some joints and then took a step back.

"Alright, let's get you going," he said, turning around to notice three jeeps coming for them.

The crew went forward and got into the jeeps. Dr. Brown opened the driver seat door and got inside. He then waited for everybody else to board before driving off and leading the others behind as they went on the road towards the launch site.

Tristan sat with his helmet in his lap. It was nighttime, but still warm and bright due to so many artificial lights around. It may as well have been daytime as they got closer to the launch pad. Tristan focused on the Lindworm as they got closer and closer and she got bigger and bigger. The actual shuttle was not that big, but it was the external storage tanks and booster rockets that gave it a grand appearance.

Dr. Brown drove up to the lift going up to the access service arm through the mobile launcher. Everybody in the jeep got out and made their way to the corridor leading to the elevator. The other two jeeps pulled up behind theirs and everybody from their separate teams, with the exception of the engineers, got out. Madonna was with Charlie Team and moved to join the others before turning around to face everybody else.

Tristan looked over to Bravo Team who was dressed and ready for their deployment later on. Diana wore an advanced armor suit that incorporated stealth camouflage technology. The suit went up and over her head with a hood. The entire suit was a dark black and didn't provide much protection. Only Sergeant Mendez wore a similar suit. Agent Black was dressed in her suit and Lieutenant Carse wore his original jumpsuit.

Agent Black made her approach to the astronauts with Charlemagne.

"Take care out there," Charlemagne said, shaking the hand of Captain Poulsson before moving over to Sergeant Zajaczkowski. "Take care."

Agent Black moved over to shake the hands of her comrades as Charlemagne came to Tristan. Charlemagne offered him his hand to shake. Tristan took it.

"Please, be careful up there," Charlemagne said to him with a worried voice. "You've placed me in enough fright between Diana saying you were kidnapped by the aliens and myself being told that the UFO you were in was shot down. I don't want to feel that emotion again."

"I promise you that you won't," Tristan replied to him with a bit of confidence.

"Trust your instincts. Come back alive, my boy," he said before stepping back.

Agent Black moved over to confront Tristan.

"We're expecting great things from you, Mr. Merrick. We're confident you will be able to handle this mission with swiftness and effectiveness."

"Yes, ma'am," Tristan replied, taking her hand and shaking it.

Agent Black moved out of the way and Tristan saw the other astronauts talking to their peers. Diana took the moment to come and confront Tristan.

"I guess we won't have time for anything romantic," Tristan quietly said, noticing Diana extend her hand for a handshake.

"Nope," Diana replied, taking his hand and bringing him closer for them to hug, "but that doesn't mean I won't hug you. You look like a jet pilot in this uniform."

"You look like something out of those video games you play with Moira."

The couple smiled.

"Please, be careful, Tristan," Diana quietly whispered into his ear. "And don't forget this one thing when you're up there because I'll be thinking of it when I'm down in the base. I love you."

"I love you too," Tristan whispered back.

The two parted and looked at each other. Diana looked as though she was about to cry, but she held herself as the two withdrew. Diana took a step back to stand next to Moira who simply nodded to Tristan.

"Alright, Alpha Team, get moving," Dr. Brown said.

The three of them turned around after giving their farewells and started to make their way to the elevator.

"Do not be afraid," Madonna said to Diana as she stood next to her. "I will watch over him for you."

Madonna then walked forward to join the rest of Alpha Team. She boarded the tram elevator going up and then the doors closed. Lieutenant Carse and Sergeant Mendez saluted the astronauts as the lift went up. Tristan started to take deep breaths as they were shot up into the ground before it came to a halt about one-hundred fifty-feet in the air.

"This way, Alpha Team," an engineer said, pointing down the corridor.

Alpha Team entered the access bridge and crossed it. Tristan looked outside to the bright darkness where it was hard to see down to the ground below. The crew went to the end where another engineer waited to guide them inside.

Tristan entered the space shuttle and immediately the raw nature of the craft began to take notice. It was dark inside at a shade of blue. A ladder led up to the seats in the cockpit where the remaining two engineers were to help. They helped the team into their chairs. Captain Poulsson took the principle one in the center while Tristan and Madonna were to the side and Sergeant Zajaczkowski in a seat next to her comrade. She was given the pilot seat in case the autopilot was to fail.

"Are you okay, Merrick?" Captain Poulsson asked with a smile as he looked over to him.

"Yeah, I'm good," he replied as an engineer strapped him in for the ride.

"Alpha Team, this is Charlemagne. We're still returning to command, but I'm giving this time to remind you that you have an hour and a half before you land at the landing zone. Everything will be automated, or more or less, under our control, so please do not worry if the system fails. Sit tight because the real work will come when you arrive. Your EVA suits are tucked nearby with LCG to replace the thermal suits you are currently wearing.

"Your helmet," an engineer said, passing Tristan's helmet to him.

"Thank you," Tristan replied, taking the helmet and putting it over his head.

Tristan looked through his helmet, staring up into the night sky through the cockpit windows that provide an extremely limited view. His visor was kept up, keeping his vision to his naked eye. He started to take deep breaths but refrained from doing so as he noticed that his oxygen tank had been turned on. The engineers had left the team on their own, and it was any moment until it was time to launch.

• •

"Radio check," Charlemagne said from within the operations center.

"Loud and clear," Captain Poulsson replied.

"L-minus ninety seconds," Barry said to Charlemagne as they watched the footage on screen.

Charlemagne looked up and then pressed a button on his dashboard.

"Tristan, Diana, can you hear me?"

"Copy," Tristan replied.

"Copy," Diana also said from elsewhere.

"You have no idea of how proud I am of the two of you, but I don't want there to be any pressure against either of you on this mission. You're both about to be thrusted into situations that nobody your age should have to be placed in but will be placed in given the dangerous circumstances. Millions upon millions of innocent lives will be saved by your actions today. It doesn't justify what you're doing, but the fact that the two of you volunteered for this shows the great heroic deed the two of you are about to commit. For this, I am proud."

"L-minus twenty seconds," Barry said over the radio.

Tristan noticed the engine of the rocket started to prepare itself, causing the entire vessel to vibrate. He closed his eyes before opening them again. The vibration of the craft got worse.

"Ten seconds," Barry said to Charlemagne. "Nine, eight…"

"Seven, six…" Tristan whispered to himself.

The craft shook even more violently, causing Tristan to hold on tight to the arm rests as he muttered to himself.

"Three, two… one."

"Ignition set," Barry said as he and Charlemagne watched the footage on screen.

The spacecraft shook even more at a Richter scale of magnitude eight, setting off a large explosion beneath itself as it started to make its ascent. Diana watched from the back of the room, daring to close to her eyes lest something happen. A large plumage of smoke dispersed from underneath the rocket as it flew up and away from the ground.

"And we have liftoff!" Barry said, taking a deep sigh as he looked through his glasses.

Tristan looked up to the brightness that was outside.

"Mr. Cabernet, this is Dr. Brown. The Lindworm had cleared. I repeat, the craft had cleared from her launch."

"Thank you, doctor. We'll take it from here," Charlemagne replied as Barry and the others clapped in celebration.

Diana refrained from celebrating and instead kept her eyes on the screen as she held her arms crossed. The shuttle flew off the screen, leaving behind a large storm of smoke and light that slowly dispersed.

In the spaceship, the craft began to roll as it continued to shake violently, continuing upwards and upwards with gaining speed.

"Oh, God," Tristan whispered under his breath as he continued to endure the motion.

The cockpit span with the tilt maneuver, giving the crew the same sensation they experienced during their training. Tristan closed his eyes as they continued.

Charlemagne watched from Earth as he saw the footage change to bring the Lindworm back on-screen. He watched as the ship rolled before coming out of total sight from the camera.

Tristan opened his eyes as soon as it calmed down. The cabin still shook, but inertia settled down as well as the spinning.

"Booster rockets have disengaged," Barry said over the radio. "They're all on their own now. Let's hope that the engines handle its own."

"Aye," Charlemagne replied, looking at the screen as it changed to an animation of the rocket at approximately height in the atmosphere.

"We're actually going to make it," Captain Poulsson said with returning confidence.

"You have to trust Cabernet engineering," Charlemagne replied over the radio. "We're tracking your speed and impressed with the output so far. You're reaching the peak estimated velocity. Sit back for now, enjoy the ride, and the view. The capital ship is an hour or so away."

Act 6, Scene 2

"Alright, Bravo Team," Eleanor addressed as they stood in the elevator going to the helipad. "Alpha Team are enroute to their target – ETA fifty minutes, which means that we have to get moving to hold up our end of the bargain."

Diana looked over to her and nodded. She then looked over to Moira who wore a Cabernet Space jumpsuit. Diana held a rifle in her hands, pistol in a holster on her right thigh and a dagger on her left thigh. She had her hood over her head and pulled down the face piece, which allowed her to see out.

The elevator doors opened, revealing the V-TOL still parked in the same place as where Agent Black had parked it when they arrived. The rear doors were open earlier to let them move their equipment on board and all that remained was for them to board.

Eleanor led them on, moving herself to go and take her seat at the cockpit. Lieutenant Carse went forward to take the seat next to her. Diana sat down in his own seat nearby, placing her weapon on the side for her to sit down and put her seatbelt around. Moira sat nearby, directly across from her. Mika sat down on his own close to the entrance. Sergeant Mendez sat across from him.

The engine of the V-TOL started, causing a minor vibration before a long calm. The rear doors closed, and interior lights went red to signal the ship hovering upwards.

"Everybody sitting tight?" Eleanor questioned.

"Affirmative, ma'am," Sergeant Mendez replied.

"Let's go then," she said.

The ship lifted upwards and the landing gear closed. The jet propulsion engines of the ship changed their direction, giving them a boost as the aircraft launched itself into the air and northwards.

"I have to ask," Mendez said, looking over to Mika. "Why aren't you with your comrade?"

"I'll admit, I was… divided between accompanying her and going with this team. In the end, I am here instead as it seemed the most important. My task is to protect monarchy, and what is in that vessel is within that realm."

"So, you have a monarchy then."

"At the present, no. The military council has replaced our monarch due to the threat of your species."

Oh…"

"Are you okay?" Diana asked Moira as she sat forward with a mild gloomy expression.

"I'm fine," she replied.

"You don't sound fine, and you haven't said much in the last hour or so."

"I'm just focusing on the mission," she explained. "Lots going on."

"You should be proud of yourself," Diana replied. "We wouldn't be on this mission if not for you. If all goes well, all the credit or our successes will have to go to you."

"Thanks," she said with a light smile that quickly faded.

"You nagged me about me having all the fun with the adventures, and now you're finally here with me. We're going to be fine. Don't worry if you are nervous"

"I'm not."

Silence took over the rear of the V-TOL and much of the cockpit too as Agent Black seldom spoke with Charlie Team. In the next forty minutes, that changed as the ship pivoted and started to make its descent.

"Alright, we're approaching the hangar zone. Everybody hang on," Eleanor said.

The V-TOL started to make its touchdown from above the clouds, moving in on the site.

"Let's see if this skeleton key works," Eleanor remarked. "Charlemagne, open the hangar."

"Copy," Charlemagne replied.

The crew waited and heard the creaks of a hangar door opening from outside. Eleanor kept the V-TOL hovering before bringing it down into the cavernous hangar.

"Welcome home," Lieutenant Carse said as the lights from the hangar filled the cockpit.

The aircraft shook as they touched down. Eleanor withheld from opening the rear doors as she grabbed her weapon and went into the rear. Diana unlatched her seatbelt and stood up. Mika stood up and stood in the center of the rear, revealing his limbs and boney hands to be tied together with a cable tie.

"There," Eleanor said, finishing before holding her weapon to the alien. "No hard feelings with anything I say next. It's all just acting."

"I do not have feelings," the being replied, turning around to face the door.

"Open up!" a voice shouted from outside.

"Alright, you two," Eleanor said as she the rear-door release switch. "Time to disappear."

"Copy," Diana replied, hitting a device on her wrist that caused her to vanish.

"Perfect," Eleanor smiled, looking back to the door as it finished opening. "Stand down. What is the meaning of this?"

"Don't move!" an agent in black said to her.

Diana looked ahead and could see about half-a-dozen agents with weapons pointed at them.

"What the hell is this?" the director shouted, shoving past some agents to get to Agent Black. "Where the hell have you been, woman? What the hell made you think you could show your face here again?"

"I'm eternally sorry, director," Eleanor replied. "After my interrogation with Charlemagne failed, I left with him to force him to reveal information we gravely needed. I wasn't able to communicate with you due to an error in the computer system, and my failure to take the appropriate gear with me was short-sighted. However, it was a worthwhile trek. Behold, a live capture of these alien creatures."

The director crossed his arms as he scowled at Eleanor before shifting his eyes to the alien.

"My God, they're disgusting," he said. "How did you come against this?"

"Mr. Cabernet was harboring it in a discrete location. I had to retrieve it with limited time to act, and in the process, I lost three of my men as well as Mr. Cabernet. They're all dead. I did, however, capture this little girl who is responsible for hacking into our systems. I'll need to interrogate her and learn of what she's found."

"I see, well, it is a pity that we lost some of our men, but it is less of a pity that we lost Mr. Cabernet. It will save us time forging a case against him. You two," the director said, pointing to two agents. "Escort Ms. Black down to the containment zone to have this… thing and this little girl locked away. Afterwards, we'll interrogate the being, and if nothing comes forward, autopsy the corpse."

"Understood, director," an agent replied.

"Everybody else, at ease and return to your posts.

"Yes, sir," another agent said.

Diana walked carefully down the ramp, entering the cylindrical cavern that was the G.D.P. hangar. She looked around before moving along at a walking pace behind the others.

She then looked at the various people around her and left the room to come into a hall leading towards the command center.

"Any word from our team in Tokyo?" the director asked as he continued down and into the command room.

"Yes, sir, but they haven't found much," an agent replied next to him.

"Have them look harder. There must be something there for us to focus on. Have our agents in the area move in to suppress locals."

"Yes, sir," the agent replied.

"I'll be in my office."

The elevator doors opened in the hall before the command center, letting Eleanor lead the alien with two agents that had joined them as well as Lieutenant Carse and Moira. All of them entered, letting Eleanor bring to her ear to whisper into her wrist communicator.

"Diana, Mendez, are you in the lift?" she questioned with a hush.

"I am, ma'am," Mendez quietly replied.

"Copy," Diana added, taking a space in the corner and hoping Mendez wasn't nearby.

"Good."

Diana stood vigilant as the elevator doors shut and the left began to make its descent. The elevator door was open to the exterior, resembling a cage instead of a cabin. They made their descent downwards into the bowls of the Earth, passing one floor and then stopping at the next. The cage door opened, allowing the escort to move forward. Diana waited for everybody to get off before following from behind as they went left down the corridor towards containment.

Two agents led the way, leaving Eleanor and Carse behind, but defenseless.

"Diana, move up with me if you're not already forward," Mendez said in their comms. "We'll take them from the front. Ms. Black and Carse, take them from behind afterwards."

"Copy," Diana replied, positioning herself to go around the team as they passed through a door and entered the detention center.

"In front of the second cell, move," Mendez ordered Diana.

"I'm there," Diana replied, kneeling down and readying her weapon.

"Reveal," Mendez said.

Diana hit the switch on her wrist and revealed herself with Mendez, ambushing the guards who jumped back.

"Weapons on the ground!" Mendez shouted.

The two agents dropped their guns and raised their hands up. Eleanor and Carse went behind them and forced them onto their knees before removing their earpieces and throwing them onto the floor. They smashed them with their foot and then put ties around each of their wrists.

"Macmillan, get the door for us," Eleanor said.

"You have no idea of the mistake you're making," one of the agents said as he was forced onto his feet.

"Did you tell the same thing to the director?" Eleanor questioned as she brought the two agents towards a cell, "because he's about to expose the organization and betray all that we stand for by inciting a galactic war."

"You're insane."

The door slid open, allowing Agent Black to push the two agents in and close the door behind them. She then turned around to accept one of the two rifles that were now available from Lieutenant Carse.

"Good, now then, let's get moving," Agent Black said, looking over to Diana and Sergeant Mendez.

"Consider it done," Mika replied, vanishing.

"Give your battery packs time to recharge," Eleanor said to the others. "Follow me and we'll take the lift back up. You can re-conceal once we're there."

"Copy that," Mendez replied, following Agent Black and Lieutenant Carse out of the detention center.

Bravo Team re-entered the vestibule corridor that connected with the lift. The doors opened and the party entered.

"Mika, are you well?" Eleanor questioned.

"I am fine."

"Good," she replied, closing the gate doors and setting their destination for the ground floor again. "We're almost through."

The bell dinged as they reached the ground floor.

"Cloaking," Mendez said, triggering his camouflage again.

"Cloaking," Diana repeated, doing the same.

"Be careful, everyone," Eleanor warned as the elevator doors opened.

Agent Black led the way out with Lieutenant Carse. Both of them held their rifles in a relaxed manner. They walked calmly out of the lift and started to cross the command center floor to get to the large round blast doors on the other side.

Diana followed from behind, walking in a similar calm fashion despite being concealed. She looked to her left and could see a slight shimmer of both Mendez and Mika nearby. She looked past them to observe the command center in better detail.

The room wasn't as large as she initially thought it was. It was bigger than the one Charlie Team were using in Kennte. From where Bravo Team was entering, there were a set of stairs on the immediate right that twisted up to a catwalk passing over and then back down a similar set of stairs on the opposite side of the room. Some monitors placed on the wall behind the stairs and three rows of counters with computer monitors positioned on a diagonal shape were positioned looking towards the center-back of the room for the first two, and against the stairwell on the last. The center of the command center had two long rows of counters, both separated in the middle and both looking to the center back. The entire room held a reddish-glow due to the monitors that projected red light, and the lack of any lamps made the room quite dim. The large monitor at the center-back that displayed a large map of the world was focused on the island of Japan. Various live footage windows were opened around the island, streaming the point of view of the four squad members who were deployed on the false alarm mission. The far-side of the room to where Bravo Team were walking towards was different to the opposite-side. The stairs that went to the catwalk weren't curved, and there was a counter of monitors underneath it. To the left of the stairs was a small room with a counter-desk and two computers. It had a door that was open and nothing more than that.

A railing blocked the center of the central command from where Diana and the others were walking, and in the center of this rail guard were two-steps of a small staircase that went down into the main area of the room. Bravo Team passed by this and made it to the end where the doors opened automatically for them to move on.

Diana continued along and left the command room, which was a small vestibule before the next room. The next room was small and known as the armory. It functioned like a locker room in the rear and there were racks of weapons and ammunition laid throughout. A lot of heavy weaponry and arms were stored around. The room was quiet and empty until they arrived. They quickly passed through into a small junction corridor with two-options. The first was to their left and the second in front of them. The room had metallic crates littered in each corner.

Eleanor led the way through the circular door in front of them, automatically opening to bring them into the barracks of the organization, which was two-stories tall although a single room. To their immediate left were vending machines, an arcade machine, and a counter with a coffee pot leading to another door out. In the center of this room, underneath a catwalk were some couches and armchairs as well as a pool table in the pathway to the door directly ahead of where they entered. To the rear of the room, next to the door to the left, were some more vending machines. In front of these dispensaries were more couches in a small seating area. In front of this area was a staircase going up to the catwalk. Two troops were at the pool table, and they both looked at Lieutenant Carse and Agent Black as they entered.

"Whoa, what's an agent like her doing here, Carse? And who's the girl?" the trooper questioned as he rested his cue on the side of the table.

"The daughter of one of our fallen comrades," Lieutenant Carse replied. "Poor Zajaczkowski… she didn't make it from our last mission."

"Oh, jeez… I'm sorry," the soldier replied, dropping his confident smile.

"No need to apologize," Eleanor replied. "You all know what you've signed up for when you volunteered to join."

"Of course," the other replied, stepping back as she walked past them.

Agent Black and the others went by the billiard table and towards the stairs going up to the catwalk. All of them made their way up and then turned left to go up a second set of stairs before turning right to face a final set that led to a closed rectangular door.

"Ready up," Eleanor said, placing a single foot on the first step towards the director's office.

"Copy that," Carse replied, readying his weapon as he stood next to Agent Black.

"We're right behind you," Mendez said.

"Let's end this then," Eleanor replied.

Agent Black looked down her sights and then went up the five steps. The door automatically opened for her to rush through with Carse behind her.

"Freeze!" she shouted as Diana hurried behind Mendez to get into a good position.

"What is the meaning of this?" the director questioned.

Diana rushed into the small room – the smallest of the rooms so far. Immediately ahead of them was another door, and next to this door was a small desk with two roller chairs in front, and another at the back where the director sat. The desk had a simple desktop computer, mouse and keyboard. To the right were two small monitors, and behind the director was a safe. Next to the safe was a black banner with the logo of the Global Defense Project – simply a white globe with a star behind it and dagger through the globe. Next to this banner was another door going elsewhere, and next to this door was a locker.

"Hands up!" Eleanor shouted. "Director Selebi, you are under arrest for the act of treason against the Committee, and a violation of core policies and the integrity of the Global Defense Project. Lieutenant, get Moira to the server room."

"Aye, ma'am," Carse replied, lowering her weapon from the director and looking to Moira. "Come on."

The two of them went into a doorway immediately ahead of the door they had just come in through.

"Stupid woman," the director mocked, pulling out a pistol and aiming at her.

"Not so fast," Mendez replied, revealing himself next to him.

Diana revealed herself too, but she was positioned next to Agent Black. Mendez disarmed the director, taking his pistol off of him and slamming his head into the keyboard.

"You're relieved, director," Mendez said.

Mendez lowered his weapon to put ties around the wrists of the director before showing him inside as Eleanor came around to sit in his desk.

"You are making a mistake, Ms. Black," the director warned. "You are putting all of us at risk, for what? You and your self-righteous morals. You are only delaying the inevitable by trusting these creatures."

"I am trusting my instincts, director," Agent Black replied. "You violated the code of the Global Defense Project and went behind the backs of the Committee. We are meant to conceal, not reveal."

"Foolish woman," the director laughed. "I am acting out the very wishes of our masters."

Agent Black looked at him, shook her head and then picked up a phone. She dialed a number into it, causing a screech to occur throughout the headquarters.

"Attention, this is Agent Black. Due to emergency circumstances, Director Selebi will be taking a leave of absence as the leader of the Global Defense Project. I, Agent Black, will be taking over until further notice. All staff are to cease their scheduled activities until further notice, including the current expedition to Japan. I repeat, all staff are to cease their scheduled activities until further notice. Laboratories are to be vacated immediately."

"Don't listen to her! Help! It's a coup!" the director shouted.

"Get him out of here!" Eleanor yelled to Mendez, pushing him back.

"Shut up!" Mendez remarked, picking up the director and tossing him onto the ground.

Some gunshots passed through from below.

"Looks like we've got some resistance," Mendez remarked, picking up the director and bringing him onto his right shoulder.

"Let's retreat to the server room. We need to contact the Committee and get their approval," Eleanor said, standing up and going to the door.

Diana looked from Mendez to her, and then over to the director. She held her weapon nervously as she noticed more gunshots coming from below.

"Cambridge, what are you waiting for? Let's go?" Eleanor ordered.

Diana rushed into the server room, letting Eleanor close the door behind them. The server room was a narrow room with servers lined ahead of them. About ten of them were in total. To their side was nothing, and on the opposite wall, a large screen with the G.D.P. logo and six monitors, three on each side, showing security footage.

"Do you think you can contact the Committee without my access? Good luck," the director taunted as he was thrown onto the ground.

"Don't need it," Moira replied.

"We have the best hacker on the case," Eleanor added.

"You might want to hold off on that," Mendez remarked, looking at footage from the labs.

Diana looked at the footage. She could see scientists in hazmat suits in some sort of quarantine chamber with the vessel under bright surgical lights. They were walking around the room, preparing for the vivisection.

"Why haven't they listened to me?" Eleanor complained.

The director laughed.

"Did you think they would listen to you just because you told them to? Their loyalty lies to me," the director stated.

"No, communications have been shut off to the lower levels," Moira corrected. "He saw this coming!"

Immediately after her words, the lights in the room shut off, throwing them into almost complete darkness had there not been so many monitors. An emergency orange light started to flash over the doorway instead.

"What's happening?" Moira questioned.

"Lockdown. No way out for you. You think you can take on the best soldiers humanity has to offer on your own? I think you will be needing that luck after all," the director taunted.

Eleanor growled and took cover at the doorway as troops started to move in on them. She opened fire back at them.

"What are we going to do?" Mendez questioned, taking cover behind a server.

"There's not much we can do," Eleanor replied.

"We don't have long. They're preparing for surgical operation in there," Mika said, paying close attention to the screen.

Diana looked over to Mika and then to Eleanor.

"Uh, Ms. Black?" Diana questioned. "You're not going to let that thing die in there, are you?"

"We're a little pinned down at the moment, Diana. Macmillan is working as fast as she can. Don't worry, I'm not turning around on what I promised to these aliens. I didn't come all the way here just to die."

"Right," she replied, "it's just... with all that's going on, usually someone backstabs us by now."

"Okay," Agent Black replied, ignoring her. "Diana, Mendez, you'll have to get to the labs on foot and stop them yourselves."

"The lifts will be on lockdown mode," Carse stated. "There'll be no way through."

"We'll have to go around through the back – through the medical bay," Mendez replied. "Come on."

"Alright," Diana said, taking a deep breath as she reloaded her weapon.

"I'll provide some covering fire," Eleanor said. "Get ready to run through."

"You don't have much time," Carse reported. "Looks like they're about to start any second now. It's about a quarter to four right now."

"On my mark then," Eleanor said, reloading her weapon.

Diana and Mendez concealed themselves. Mika also concealed himself.

"Go!" Eleanor shouted, opening fire.

Act 6, Scene 3

"Look at that," Poulsson said in awe.

One hour since launch, the Lindworm started to make its approach to the alien fleet as they flew over the top-most layer of the atmosphere. Compared to the Lindworm, every ship in the convoy was about one-hundred times more massive. Some stretched almost a kilometer in length. The spacecraft continued its automated approach towards the capital ship, demonstrating the enormity of these colossuses as they passed through and got closer.

Tristan watched from his seat, examining the intricate and yet quite plain design of these black beauties. He eyed the ship that he knew to be their target – the capital ship of the fleet as it stood out from the rest of them by its length. The Lindworm started to make its approach towards this ship, but quickly and suddenly, a smaller alien ship from the fleet started to make its pass in their direction, raising fear that they might crash into it as they got closer.

"Mission Control," Poulsson reported. "We've got a problem."

"What is it Alpha-One?" Charlemagne asked.

"The path you set up for us... it didn't factor in other objects passing through, did it? We've got one of the other alien ships passing by, and I think..."

Poulsson paused as he saw them making a direct line for the ship.

"Yeah, we're going to crash."

"Understood, we'll deactivate the auto pilot so you can take control," Charlemagne replied.

The Lindworm got increasingly closer to this ship. A collision was imminent.

Poulsson pressed in some buttons and caused the ship to slow down.

"Alright, everybody hold on," Poulsson said.

The Lindworm tilted upwards and away from the ship, pointing up to the underside of another ship.

"Get out of the way!" Zajaczkowski shouted.

"Sorry!" Poulsson replied, steering them clear and under the hull.

Various sensors from the craft started to trigger, but then they calmed down as they made their way off.

"Watch for that debris," Zajaczkowski said. "It's filthy up here."

"Calm down," Poulsson remarked. "I know what I'm doing."

"And don't forget to land us at our target," she added with a smirk.

Tristan looked back at the capital ship and watched as Poulsson flew them to the landing zone. The spaceship made its approach, tilting its path as it started to fly away from the capital ship before going back towards it to land on the side, just below the open bow.

"Nice and easy," Zajaczkowski said, bracing herself as she tightened her grip around the arm rests of her chair.

Tristan bit down on his tongue, waiting for the inevitable impact as they touched the surface of the behemoth next to them. The entire spacecraft shook before triggering vibrations as the ship slowed down before coming to a stop.

"Activating the magnetic locks," Poulsson stated before unlatching his seatbelt. "Mission Control, this is Alpha-One."

"Go ahead, Alpha-One."

"We've made it to the target location and are moving out," Poulsson reported.

"Copy that, Alpha-One. Proceed with caution," Charlemagne advised.

Tristan unlatched his seatbelt, releasing him to go to the back of the flight deck where four suits, one of them specialized for Madonna, waited for them. Poulsson and Zajaczkowski met Tristan at the back of the cockpit with Madonna. He removed his helmet and placed it on the ground, only to see it hit the ground and then bounce up slowly. He quickly grabbed it and looked around for a place to put it. The cockpit was divided into two sections in the rear. One the right were EVA suits and three assault rifles to strap around and bring with them, and to the left, a place to put their ACE suits.

Everybody, along with Tristan, undressed and re-dressed into the proper gear. It was much easier putting on the necessary equipment and under-garments in space than on Earth. Poulsson double-checked Tristan's suit to ensure it was properly secured. Zajaczkowski checked Poulsson's, and he checked hers. Madonna wore a similar suit over her body, in addition to her cloak, which she wore overtop.

A big difference between these suits to the ones used in practice was the application of an oxygen tank alongside a jetpack to aid with movement. They didn't receive any training with the jetpack and were advised to be cautious with it.

Captain Poulsson readied the cargo bay for their extraction by raising the doors. The area was already oxygen depleted and all that was left was for them to get moving. Poulsson made his way to the door of the airlock, opening it and letting Zajaczkowski through first before Madonna and then Tristan.

The airlock doors closed behind him, and in the next second, the shutter in front of him opened to let him push himself out, grabbing hold of the side before coming out and holding onto a handle bar that went around. The doors closed behind him, and he waited with Zajaczkowski and Madonna for Poulsson to come through. Tristan looked up, causing his eyes to widen as he looked at the starry emptiness of space above him as they were officially in the great void. He brought a hand forward and in front of him, waving it in front of him, he felt what it was like to be in a weightless and airless system.

Tristan held onto a bar tightly as he moved himself over, giving space for Poulsson to come through. Captain Poulsson hit a switch for the airlock to close before letting him move along as they all looked to Zajaczkowski in front. She led the way up a ladder that brought them to the edge of the shuttle cargo hold. She vaulted over and brought herself over to hang on the rim to stop down onto the wing of the Lindworm.

Madonna followed before Tristan could get up and over, lowering his feet down the ladder and touching down before turning around. The blackness of the capital ship showed around them, in addition to her size and sleekness. The surface of the ship composed of a certain unidentifiable metal which was fashioned together in hexagon shapes. The Lindworm landed on a slope that required them to cross before going up and over to reach the exterior bow.

Tristan looked up and out of the Lindworm as he reached over the edge of the shuttle cargo hold. He could see out and beyond to the great large sphere ahead of him – Earth, like a great blue marble. From here, they looked down onto the North American continent where it was dark and the various connection of lights from city to city lit up the surface of the Earth like a tree. Over the Earth was a thin layer of clouds that was transparent. Along the horizon was a view of the rising sun in the east. Tristan was sure not to stare directly at it. He looked back down and re-concentrated on the mission.

"We'll have to use our jetpacks to make the vault over the capital ship," Zajaczkowski suggested, lowering herself onto the rim of the wing. "I don't see any other way up and over."

"You're right," Poulsson said. "If we're careful, we can grab on and shoot ourselves back down."

"I see what you are suggesting and I agree," Madonna replied as she lowered herself down.

Tristan took a deep breath before lowering himself down. He looked over to where they had to get to and started to move slowly. Zajaczkowski made it to the edge of the wing that brought them closest to where they needed to go. She then eased herself down before pushing herself off to gloat towards the vertical surface that they had to traverse.

Madonna did a similar maneuver, gliding blissfully from the wing to the wall, taking position with Zajaczkowski as they waited for the others. Tristan made it to the edge of the wing and looked at where he was and then over to where he needed to be before pushing himself and letting physicals take over as he was brought to the others.

Tristan gently crashed into the side of the capital ship, letting himself turn his back against the vertical surface before looking over to Poulsson who came around. Once they were reunited, all that remained was the trick maneuver.

"Alright, I know we haven't practiced this in person, but we still know how to operate these things," Poulsson said in reference to the jetpacks.

Tristan found the switch on his wrist, turning it on to engage the boosters in his backpack through a deep switch on the temple of his helmet. He took a deep breath and looked to the others as they readied. Tristan brought a finger to his temple, steadily holding it over the switch with trembling hands before looking over to the others as they engaged. He closed his eyes and did the same, launching himself up with a simple boost before turning his body to grab the rim of the bow. He faced where he wanted to grab and extended his hands over, but instead of swiping the rim, he instead swiped at nothing and found himself floating up and away.

"Tristan!" Poulsson shouted, looking over to him as Tristan started to panic.

Poulsson shot himself up and towards Tristan instead of towards the others as Tristan panicked and struggled to position himself to the bow of the ship. Poulsson grabbed him, putting an arm around his waist and steering them to face the others before shooting them towards the bow, causing them to land against the surface and drift to the side slightly before hitting the side of some sort of device on the bow.

"Jeez, thanks," Tristan remarked, feeling his heart point as he sat on the bow for a moment.

"Alright, Madonna, we're on the ship. What now?"

A deep shouting of a foreign sound caught their attention. Alpha Team looked over to where three bulk aliens made their approach to them in a green armor and helmet that covered their faces. They were anthropoid, but large and tall – about the same height as Madonna.

Compared to Madonna, these aliens had a larger amount of muscle mass than her, assuming she had any muscles. Their bulkiness didn't arise from their suits either. The beings didn't carry weapons, although at closer glance, it appeared as though they had some sort of wrist-mounted devices that might project something as they pointed their fists towards them. The beings shouted at them in a strange and foreign language of sounds and dark pitches. Poulsson, Zajaczkowski and Tristan took their guns and pointed them back at them.

Madonna floated towards them and raised an open palm. For the first time, she spoke in a different language through her translator. Whoever these troopers were, they weren't of the same race or species as her. The alien troopers lowered their fists, although they didn't really have any fingers or even hands. Madonna then faced the crew.

"We are secure. Lower your weapons," Madonna said. "We are to be escorted to the bridge where the military command awaits me and my report."

"Let's not keep them waiting then," Poulsson replied, lowering his gun and looking over to the others as they stepped aside for Madonna to lead forward.

Alpha Team was led by three green men towards a type of airlock where they were allowed to rest for a moment as (some) gravity returned. It was terrestrial, but enough to keep them on the ground. Madonna removed her helmet and suit, returning to wear her cloak.

"The composition of gases is safe for your species," Madonna said. "It contains a degree of what I believe your species need to breath."

"She's right," Poulsson said.

"What about microscopic organisms or diseases?" Tristan asked, hesitant to remove himself from the suit.

"Our ships are sterile, but I see your concern," Madonna replied. "You have little to fear in terms of your own diseases. After all, I have been on your planet and have not had any problem so far."

Tristan nodded and turned off his oxygen. The entire team undressed from their EVA suits to stand in their jumpsuits. Due to the liquid-coolant systems that ran underneath their suits, it was hard to know what the exact temperature of the ship was, although, a cool wind that blasted around the airlock told Tristan that it was cold.

Once everybody was ready, the doors opened for them to enter the interior of the capital ship and be led by four aliens that were similar to Madonna in terms of their structure but dressed in dark grey robes like Mika.

The beings did not speak with Madonna, unless they did and she just didn't reply, or they were speaking in their own method of communication. They were led through the craft and brought up to the bridge, which was a set-up straight from a science fiction move. The bridge of the enormous ship was also similar to the flight deck of Mike's spaceship that Tristan was aboard earlier, except it was larger and more expansive. There were also more aliens of the same species as Madonna, but in different colored cloaks, working around with holographic monitors.

Madonna was brought forward to the center where she stood with the rest of Alpha Team and their escorts. The other aliens were calm. Tristan kept an eye on them.

"Where is the Council?" Madonna asked, turning to one of her escorts.

The alien she was talking to stepped forward and raised its right hand to the left. A holographic display appeared in front of Madonna, letting her look forward at what appeared to be a committee of twelve other aliens like her, except they wore white robes.

One of the commands started to talk in a language similar to the one spoken by the anthropoids, but it was made of certain pitches and tones of sounds that appeared to project from the aliens themselves instead of a translator.

"Authorities on the world below have secured the lost vessel," Madonna's translator said, talking over a similar pitch and tone of sounds that came organically from her. "I require transportation to bring myself down and have the vessel returned with my guardian."

The beings in the display replied to her.

"There will be no war, admiral," Madonna's translator responded. "I will not allow you bring our species to extinction or cause the collapse of our empire."

The beings then replied.

"These are the Great Ones that have sacrificed their lives to have me return to this vessel – the Great Ones are not our enemies. It is our duty to the Almighty to protect them, not destroy them."

The beings in the hologram replied to her once more. The green anthropoids pointed their weapons towards Madonna and the escorts, causing the aliens in grey cloaks to reveal staffs from their cloaks and point them towards the anthropoids.

"I demand that you cease this abuse of your power, admiral," Madonna stated.

The admiral replied in their native language before transmissions cut-off and Madonna turned around to face the soldiers.

"What's going on?" Poulsson asked, holding his weapon with extra caution as he eyed the troopers.

"The Council has seized power and deemed my efforts to be a failure. They have defected and sworn loyalty to Beliyal. The fleet is being positioned to strike at your urban centers. I have been placed under arrest for my failure. It is over."

"Like hell it is," Poulsson replied, raising his gun up and firing at one of the green troopers.

"Stop!" Madonna shouted.

Poulsson fired at the trooper, grazing its armor, but doing barely any penetrable damage. One of the aliens in a grey cloak brought its staff in front of Poulsson, getting him to stop firing.

The others brought their staffs towards the green aliens as they reacted. The anthropoid that Poulsson had attacked fired its wrist-mounted cannon down into the ground as it started to scream in pain over whatever the escorts were doing. A large hole was created in the ground from the power of the cannon, one that would surely have done serious and permanent damage to Poulsson had he been hit.

Tristan looked down at awe and knew that it was certainly over for them.

Act 6, Scene 4

"Covering fire!" Agent Black shouted, firing her rifle with Lieutenant Carse down through the director's office and catwalk below.

Diana, Mendez, and Mika rushed through under the guise of their cloaks, rushing through the director's office and causing Agent Black and Lieutenant Carse to momentarily let them through. Several agents were outside, knelt at the catwalk as they formed a line to breakthrough into the server room and office. Diana followed Mendez past them, dodging a line of more agents that had just arrived to join the others.

"Keep moving! Flush them out!" an agent shouted.

The three of them passed down the stairs and made their way into an open space in the barracks to avoid bumping into any of the agents that were accumulating below. It was hard to keep track of the agents with the dim lighting and flashing yellow light. It was especially hard for Diana to see where Mendez was going.

"Keep up, you two. I'm at the back of the room," he reported.

"Copy that," Diana replied, rushing over and seeing a brief glimmer of his stealth camouflage to notice that it was Mendez next to the circular shutter doorway.

The shutters opened to reveal a fresh deployment of three soldiers. Another three passed them and went into the corridor they had just exited.

"Follow me, behind where these three are going," Mendez said, moving out of cover to run behind them.

"I'm with you," Diana replied, turning around to try and see where Mika was. "Mika, are you with us?"

"I'm focusing on your cerebral activities, Diana. I can see you just as well as I could when you weren't concealed."

"Okay…" Diana muttered, coming to the end of the corridor with Mendez.

The corridor was simple, dark, and led to a stairwell going down one-level.

"Is this the medical bay?" Diana questioned as they went down the stairs.

"No, below the barracks is the gym. There's one more level (this one) and then we're at the pub and medical facility."

"Alright," Diana replied.

"Let them through and stick back," Mendez said, taking cover at the doorway as the troopers rushed through.

Diana stuck back and then followed Mendez as he went forward again. They entered a large room similar to the barracks upstairs, but with no stairway or catwalk and treadmills and weight machines instead of couches and vending machines. The group of three ahead of them were already on the other side as they entered. An additional group of three entered at the shutters at the end and began to converse with them.

Mendez hurried along, coming to the group before stepping back as she noticed the efferent group coming towards them.

"Oof," Diana said, falling backwards as Mendez knocked into them.

"Dammit!" Mendez remarked as Diana revealed.

"Hey! Who are you?!" a trooper in the efferent group shouted, pointing at Diana.

Mendez revealed himself and immediately engaged one of the efferent agents in close-quarter combats, disarming him. He was able to take apart the soldier's weapon and then use him as a shield against the others.

"Get into cover!" Mendez shouted to Diana.

Diana rolled out of the way and attempted to re-conceal herself, but it was too soon and the batteries needed time to charge. She crawled under a bench and took cover behind a stack of weights, readying her weapon to fire. Mendez has already shot somebody onto the ground, not killing him, but badly wounding him. Mika appeared to take hold of the other, causing him to panic and fire randomly in the air.

Mendez tossed the agent he was using as cover aside and rushed into some new cover aside some lockers as they focused at the other groups as they engaged them. Diana opened fire, but these agents appeared to have found themselves some good and full cover, bringing them into a stalemate.

Mika dropped the agent he had handled onto the ground and re-concealed with ease.

"Dammit, we don't have time for this!" Mendez shouted, firing back at the troops.

Diana turned around and noticed a group of three in brown jumpsuits had just arrived.

"Oh no," Diana said, watching them rush over to them.

"Open fire!" one of them said.

Diana ducked her head in fear of being shot, but nothing happened. She raised her head up and saw that they were firing at the agents instead.

"Cease fire!" a soldier yelled, kneeling next to Diana. "Don't worry, we're on your side. We're going to do what we can to help Agent Black. Get to the labs, we'll take over from here."

"You're a lifesaver, boys," Mendez said, activating his stealth camouflage. "Come on, let's go."

Mendez rushed to the rear of the gym to get out of the line of fire. Diana activated her camouflage and went after him. They quickly ducked into cover behind the reinforcements and made their way down to another floor, reaching a type of bar.

"I hate to bother you, but the surgical procedure is starting," Agent Black said over the radio. "It's now or never."

"We're almost there, ma'am. Give us another minute," Mendez pleaded.

"Time is not mine to give, sergeant."

The team went past the bar. Mendez jumped over a counter and to the other side where another door on the same wall as the stairwell door led into a restricted section – the medical center. Diana followed Mendez through this room, which was simple. There were various hospital stretchers in rows with curtains between them. To the right, from the entrance, was a corridor leading down towards other rooms. Mendez passed them to instead hurry to the end where another circular shutter door stood in the way from them and the labs.

Mendez revealed himself, hitting his hand on the closed door as it refused to open.

"What the hell?! What's wrong with this damn thing?!" Mendez questioned.

Diana revealed herself and stood next to Mendez as he brought a finger to his ear.

"Bravo-One, I'm at the doors to the labs, but they're shut and not opening. What's going on?" Sergeant Mendez questioned, pacing around with fury and anxiety.

Eleanor didn't immediately reply.

"Look," Diana said, pointing to a panel next to the door that had been smashed.

"Unbelievable," Mendez replied.

"Bravo-Three, we're investigating the cause, but frankly don't have time to faff with the door. Find another way in on the double," Agent Black replied.

"Another way in…?" Mendez questioned, taking a step back with the upmost disbelief.

"The security panel on the side's been smashed to pieces," Diana reported in detail. "What other ways could there be?"

"Let me try and override the lock. Give me a minute," Moira replied.

Diana looked around, hearing the sound of a drill inside to cause her to become flushed with anger and fear. He eyed a series of ducts in the ceiling over the patient beds and noticed that it went straight into the wall of the laboratories.

"Not fast enough," Diana said, rushing forward and climbing atop of one of the stretchers. "I think I have something."

Mendez watched as Diana climbed atop of the bed.

"Give me a hand," Diana requested, jumping up to try and open an access gate with her rifle.

Diana opened fire at the vent and caused the gate to fly open. The sound of metal falling onto the ground sounded behind them over the sound of a drill readying to cut into the densest and toughest metal known to man and take a life. Mendez climbed up onto the bed and brought his palm to Diana, bringing another palm over it to help give her a boost up. She took it and climbed into the duct, reaching out to take her rifle with her. She then started to climb through, turning left into the laboratories.

The air ducts were dark, dusty, and extremely tight. Thankfully, she was the right size to slip through. They shook with her movement and seemed as though they were about to collapse any second now. Diana carried on, coming to a three-way intersection between going forward and to the right. She chose the right because of the light that poured through – not flashing light, but a bright white light at the end of the grate. She made it to the end and started to punch a fist at the grate to get it to open. She saw the operating room below, but they were in an isolated glass chamber with the rock on a table and drill lowering down as it started to make its incision into the vessel.

"No!" Diana shouted. "No!"

Her screams were of no use. None of the scientists inside could hear her. They were all inside the operating chamber.

Diana continued to pound on the grate, but it was no use. She then brought her hands to try and fit her gun in front of her to use it to bash the grate open, but her movement caused the duct to give up and collapse. She then fell onto the floor where she quickly recovered, picked up her weapon and ran over to get the attention of the scientists. Diana fired her rifle into the air to try and get the attention of the scientists. It was no use. She then aimed her shots into the glass, causing it to shatter and pieces to collapse down.

The scientists in hazmat suits turned around in shock and horror as they saw Diana aiming her weapon towards them. They all put their hands up.

"Stop that drill!" Diana warned them.

One of the scientists turned off the drill and then resumed to keep his hands up.

"Get out of the chamber," Diana ordered.

The scientists began to move over to the door and open it. They then slowly poured out. Behind Diana, the doors into the medical facility opened and Mendez and Miko entered. Mendez and Diana kept their weapons trained on the scientists as Miko went around to examine the meteorite vessel.

"It is intact," Mika reported to Diana.

Diana turned to Mendez and gave a thumbs up.

"Thank God," Mendez breathed, raising a finger to his ear. "Charlie-One, this is Bravo-Three. We have secured the package. Tell the Alpha boys to meet us outside. It's over..."

"Copy that, Bravo-There. Stand-by... we have yet to hear from Alpha Team. We will inform you of any developments. Good work," Charlemagne replied.

Diana looked over to Mika and started to laugh with relief as it was all over on their end. Mendez joined in, lowering his weapon at the scientists who stood back, lowering their trembling hands.

Act 6, Scene 5

"Come in Alpha-One," Charlemagne said over the radio. "Alpha Team, do you copy?"

"We've lost contact with Alpha," Barry said, turning to face Charlemagne.

"Impossible. What could have happened? Their mission was simple – return Madonna to the capital ship."

"I'll go check for possible jamming or interruptions on the radar outside," Barry said, standing up. "I'll be back. Don't win this one without me."

"Oh, don't be so confidence," Charlemagne replied, looking over to him as he passed him at the back of the room. "We haven't won this yet."

• •

"It can't be over," Tristan pleaded. "You're the most intelligent being I have ever met. You must know of something, anything, to stop this war."

"I know of another method," Madonna affirmed. "The Council will do all that they can in their power to stop us, especially as we attack and widen their power. I spoke to them, and they deemed my efforts to be a failure. The Council argued that in bringing you three aboard, I have revealed too much. They are using that violation as an excuse to advance their goals to wipe out your planet. They have defected. Guardians, remove the weapons from these soldiers and prepare these Great Ones for combat."

"Yes," a guardian replied, walking over to the unconscious bodies of the anthropoids.

Each of them took the devices mounted around the wrists of the soldiers. They were then brought to Poulsson, Zajaczkowski and Tristan.

"How do you use these?" Poulsson questioned, checking the device out.

"With limited function," Madonna replied. "These are designed for our genetically-enhanced infantry, to be used with the help of their helmets. All you can do is press the manual trigger at the front.

"Oh…" Poulsson replied. "Doesn't seem that advanced to me."

"Each device can overheat with overuse, causing your limbs to set on fire or explode," Madonna warned. "Use with extreme caution. Aim to fire a concentrated burst of highly-energetic projectiles at hostiles as we go through."

"I… I don't think I should be using one of these," Tristan remarked, feeling nervous with the immense weight at his wrist.

The weapon was almost too heavy for him to lift his arm. He could tell the others were having a similar discomfort as they tested their aim by using their other hand to stabilize their arms.

A guardian spoke to Madonna in their language.

"I see," Madonna replied, turning to Alpha Team. "We need to leave now. Reinforcements have been deployed to secure the bridge. I need your help to reach the Host. Once there, I can restore power to the throne by communicating with the rest of the Host."

"Just lead the way and we'll have your back," Poulsson replied.

"Let us move then," Madonna said, moving to face the guardians. "Protect this bridge with your lives."

Madonna then turned away from the guardians and began to make her way out of the bridge. Alpha Team followed, moving with her to a cabin that resembled an elevator shaft. It took them down at a fast pace, opening on the opposite side to reveal a long central corridor that led to another elevator.

The tunnel was dark grey with a flat surface on the ground and cylindrical shape all around to the end. Various tubes and contraptions were found on the side, but the general shape was tubular. Some banners with synthetic red fabric could be seen hung at some places. A group of four anthropoids had entered from a door on the side and proceeded to yell in a deep and loud tone.

"I'd suggest that you conceal yourself," Poulsson warned, rushing forward to take cover behind some crates.

"No use. Their visors would see right through me," Madonna replied, taking cover next to Tristan at a large contraption to the left.

Poulsson took the first shot at the aliens with his new weapon, causing the entire arm of a being to rip-off, spilling a dark greenish-brown liquid. The being shouted in pain, and then fell forward onto the floor. They returned fire, causing massive damage around.

Zajaczkowski and Poulsson returned fire. Tristan didn't dare to look as he stayed in hiding. The others pushed forward.

"Hurry, we must move on before more arrive," Madonna said to Tristan, moving from their cover to rush behind the others.

Tristan stood up and went forward. It was easier to run with the level of gravity in the ship, but unfortunately, this wasn't their natural environment compared to the hordes of green-armored anthropoids. Another group appeared ahead through some doors to the side, forcing Alpha Team to dig in and find some new cover.

Tristan ducked into the prone position and tried to see if he could help. He took some shots from a crate at whatever he could see, leaving the rest to the expert sharpshooters. Tristan aimed and almost grazed an alien. He then withdrew and stopped from participating as the others went forward.

"Hallway – clear!" Poulsson shouted, vaulting over a crate.

Tristan stood up and saw the spillage of what must've been their blood, or a similar liquid used for the same purpose – blood. He leaped over the wounded bodied and continued along, turning his neck to take one last look at the bodies with uneasiness. Tristan then continued on and ducked into some new cover he found himself. He was too distracted by the chaos ahead of him to fire back.

"Clear! Move up!" Poulsson shouted again, vaulting over his cover.

Tristan kept his eyes focused on the aliens on the ground. He took deep breaths as he continued forward and ran with the others to another lift. Madonna joined them before she put her hand on the panel to lower the carriage.

"Are you okay, Tristan?" Poulsson asked, removing his weapon for a moment as he knelt down.

"Yeah, it's just… I'm not sure how I feel about all this…" Tristan replied with a straight face. "It's new to me."

"I understand," Poulsson replied. "It's not easy for any of us. Just take deep breaths and keep up, okay?"

"Copy," Tristan responded, nodding.

Poulsson picked up his device and placed it over his forearm. Alpha Team arrived to another room, or corridor, which was circular with a device in the middle aiming upwards. Long steps going upwards surrounded the center at three layers before coming up to four different exits. Alpha Team stood at one of them, which was the lift. A ceiling covered the steps, but not the wide large center. The entire structure was mysterious, but they had little time to investigate as more soldiers arrived to pin them down from above. Tristan could see them on the other side, on the balcony.

"The way to the Host is just past here. We have little left to go," Madonna said.

"Contact!" Poulsson said, kneeling to take a shot.

Zajaczkowski rushed forward and took a graze on her arm as he took cover at a column. She returned fire. Tristan took the chance to rush over and take cover at another column. He then looked over to Zajaczkowski's injury, which was a singe mark on her jumpsuit. Madonna stood with Tristan.

Tristan tried to peak around the corner, seeing if he could try to help out again. Shots came towards him, causing him to peak out from the other side. He took some blind shots and then kept hidden again.

"We're thinning them out – push on!" Poulsson shouted.

Tristan popped out and ran to the next column with Madonna. He then did the same again so that he was at the next one. The others followed from behind. He did the same again, hiding and then going. Anthropoid soldiers continued to drop down from above as he moved to the next pillar. Zajaczkowski and Poulsson fire at them until little remaining the room. Tristan went to another pillar and fired randomly into the chamber.

Projectiles passed Tristan, maiming the wall ahead of him and the pillar he stood behind. The effect of these weapons on the tough-structure of the capital ship showed the total strength of the weapons. The projectiles were able to rip through the alloy like paper, leaving behind smoldering holes and dents. Tristan looked past to see the condition of the area. There were many corpses on the ground in the center of the chamber. Aliens continued to drop down, finding themselves shot immediately by the others.

Tristan took the opportunity to run to the last pillar, meeting Poulsson as he joined from the other end.

"These beings aren't the smartest," Poulsson remarked, taking a moment to let his weapon cool down. "Tristan, pass me your cannon if you're not going to use yours."

Tristan removed his and slid it to Poulsson who attached it. Madonna made her way forward to a glowing barrier, or a doorway, that led into the next room. She stood in the center and looked back at the onslaught.

"Tell me, Madonna, is there any other way into where we're about to go to?" Poulsson questioned, popping out of cover to continue laying fire. "I haven't seen any come through from there, but I'm seeing a whole lot come from everywhere else."

"No, this entrance leads to the Host and is a one-way route," Madonna said. "We must go now."

"You go," Poulsson replied, moving back into cover, "with Tristan. Zajaczkowski and I will hold here. Just go and please, stop the war!"

"I apologize that it had to come to this," Madonna simply remarked. "Thank you, Great Ones."

Madonna disappeared through the force field, leaving Tristan with Poulsson. Zajaczkowski moved next to Tristan and continued to lay down fire.

"Don't wait up, Merrick. Move!" Poulsson shouted.

"I'm going," Tristan replied, running through the barrier as Poulsson gave him some covering fire.

The force field was similar to the transparent field aboard Mike's spaceship. It tickled him as he went through, but took him to a short corridor that led to a type of long catwalk over a pit in the floor. At the end was another force field. Madonna had already made it to the end. Tristan rushed over to follow her. They then passed through the force field together, finding themselves in a similar room that led to another doorway. This doorway led to another hall, leading them onwards to another one, and then another one until they finally reached something different.

The two of them entered a small corridor, one that was narrower and shorter than the others. The walls were a different color too. It was Martian red. Madonna went forward to the end where a single force field waited for them to pass. Madonna moved forward, stopping for a moment in front of the barrier before bringing herself through. Tristan did the same, pausing for a moment before entering into the extremely dark room on the other side.

Tristan looked around and felt as though he was in limbo. It looked as though he was in a large pit with darkness that extended for miles on either side. The only exception was that at his feet was another, harder force field that pulsated with energy at where his feet stood. The platform he and Madonna walked on was hexagonal. The bluish glow that pulsated in the middle of the glass met itself like waves as it centered in the very middle of the platform. Madonna made her way to the very middle of the platform. She went slowly as Tristan lagged behind her, looking around as he continued to examine the fine details of the room before he looked to the alien.

Madonna had knelt down at the center, causing the blue pulse of energy to shift outwards instead of inwards. A large holographic screen started to appear at every single side of the platform, projecting Madonna as she looked forward and towards the screen in front of her.

"Subjects of our great empire, listen to your archon. In this moment, I have been displaced by the leaders of our Council in what they have deemed to be a necessary seizure of power in order to declare war on the Great Ones. They threaten our structure, our survival, and our empire out of a reckless fear that is the remnant emotions of our primitive ancestors. We are the enlightened ones designed to protect life and serve the Almighty. And in this moment, failure and vice have returned to these once noble subjects and thrusted them to defy me and risk our annihilation; Beliyal has entered into them. I hereby order their arrest and immediate exile. I also order the armed forces to stand down and cease hostilities against the Great Ones that have offered their lives for the survival of my own simple life."

Tristan looked at the projection of the alien archon and then back at Madonna.

"You're their ruler?" Tristan whispered to himself.

"Subjects, our collective mission persists to protect and guard innocent life, even at the cost of our own. The Great Ones will survive, and we too will survive. Our mission is not to wipe out an entire system of species and beings as our military leaders – these fallen – wish, but to protect them, especially when one of these species houses great and amazing gifts and talents. The Great Ones are meant to be protected, and we will not harm them like these fallen leaders have chosen to do. Hail to the Great Ones and let us hail the heroes that have saved both of our worlds, in the name of the Almighty."

The projection changed to display subjects, specifically those aboard the ship as they stopped fighting and instead kneeled down in loyalty. Madonna stood up, brought her arms under her cloak, and then turned around to face Tristan.

"It is done," she said.

"Holy Mother of … you're their queen? All this time, you never said anything, but you were their monarch…"

"I am not a queen; my role in the empire is one of leadership, like Mika, but of the leadership of the entire Host as royal vizier, the archon, on behalf of our true queen, the Great One I was entrusted to protect. I am the only female of our species, for that specific role," Madonna stated. "We must communicate with your own leadership at once and learn the status of the other mission."

"Right away," Tristan replied, following the archon out.

• •

"Charlie-One, this is Alpha-Four, can you hear me?" Tristan asked over the radio.

"Tristan!" Charlemagne remarked, picking up his headset immediately as he held his head over the desk in defeat.

"We're done over here. We've secured transport back to Earth and I can report there's no threat of invasion. What about on the other end?"

"Copy, Alpha-Four," Charlemagne responded. "Bravo Team is cleared and waiting for you atop of the rendezvous point. They have the package ready for your pickup."

The operations center erupted into celebration as they heard Tristan's confirmation.

"Tristan, I'm proud of you. The both of you," Charlemagne said.

"Thanks, Charles. We'll see you over in Alaska. Over and out."

"Oh, thank God it's over," Judith remarked, embracing Charlemagne from behind.

"Yes," Charlemagne replied, tapping her hand before standing up.

The two faced each other as the other engineers cheered and clapped. Judith looked at Charlemagne with a shy smile as they looked at each other and then she kissed him.

Charlemagne was pleasantly shocked and surprised by the sudden move, but he accepted it before his awareness kicked in to the operation center door opening. He parted from her and looked over to where Barry was standing and looking at them. Barry looked back at them and then left without a word. The couple looked back at him with sunken faces over the betrayal of an old friend.

Epilogue

Tristan pushed himself through the force field of the spaceship he had ridden down from the capital ship, finding himself in the twilight of a forest in southern Alaska. He looked around, feeling the coldness of the air that brushed against his face. He also tapped his feet on the earthy soil as he returned to terrestrial gravity. Poulsson and Zajaczkowski were behind him alongside Madonna and her guardians in addition to six red-armored anthropoid aliens.

All of them found themselves in the middle of a forest, facing a similar group that waited for them. About twelve agents in black stood with four soldiers in vested armor. Two scientists were with them, and they had the vessel on a platform with wheels. Moira, Agent Black, Mika, and Diana were with the crowd that faced the spaceship. A third vehicle, the second V-TOL, flew over with Charlie Team aboard. It landed and the doors opened for them to join the rest of the party. Each of them made their way over to the other and began to talk as the bureaucracy of peace took over. Tristan snuck past the crowd, taking Diana by her hand to leave the mob and find some privacy not too far, but not too close for them to embrace.

Tristan was filled with so much happiness inside himself that he tightened his grip around Diana, picking her up and spinning around with her before letting go to look back at each other.

"I don't want to ever go back up into space, ever," Tristan remarked to her as she smiled at him.

"Hey, you volunteered to go up there in the first place," Diana replied, smiling.

Tristan brought a hand to her cheek and they continued to smile at each other before being interrupted by the clearing of one's throat nearby. The two of them turned, looking over to Moira who had her arms crossed.

"Why don't you two just kiss?" Moira questioned, forcing them to drop their smiles and split apart.

"What do you mean?" Tristan replied.

"I mean kiss, like the way you two kissed the other day before bed. That's what I mean, Tristan," Moira responded in a fierce tone.

Tristan's cheeks flushed and he looked away. He looked to the side and cleared his own throat. He then took a deep breath.

"Why wouldn't you tell me?" Moira asked Diana in a defeated voice. "I trusted you with something, and you didn't feel like you could trust me?"

"Moira..."

"It's my fault, not hers," Tristan replied. "You placed her in a difficult position because I told her not to tell anyone about... about this."

"What's 'this?'" Moira questioned.

"The relationship I'm in," Tristan clarified. "I'm in a relationship with Diana. She's my girlfriend and I love her. I've been in love with her for almost the last year and the only reason everything that happened last spring happened was because I was too stupid to open myself up and confront the woman I was so heavily attracted to and had feelings for. I was hurting her... when she felt the same way I did about her, but I didn't understand her because I'm just a man."

Tristan had tears at his eyes. His body was shaking as he looked at Diana with focused eyes.

"Don't be mad at her but be mad at me. I'm the one that told her not to tell anyone of what we are, because... I mean, it's strange. And nobody knows except you, and I wanted it to stay that way because it's so hard – but we don't want to be judged for something that's innocent. It is innocent. And the only reason that I'm okay with you knowing now is if it'll mean you stay friends with her, because you mean a lot to her and I've already lost my own best friend to know that it sucks and I don't want her placed in that same situation. Please, be mad at and punish me, not Diana. Diana did nothing wrong."

Moira didn't reply and instead simply walked off. She then turned around and looked at Tristan with angry eyes. She didn't say anything and continued on her path away from them.

Tristan watched her go before looking over to Diana. He hadn't noticed that she had grabbed his hand. She then wiped the tears from his eyes and hugged him.

A moment passed and the two then calmly parted as they were faced by the tall and looming beings that were well-known to them by now. It was Mika, the chief guardian, and Madonna the Archon. Madonna faced Diana and Mika faced Tristan.

"You two have done well to show me how it is, and why it is that you are referred to as Great Ones by our elders," Madonna said. "You hold a deep power within you, Tristan. In your will to move forward, I could see what motivated you and where you were able to turn weakness into strength. It was curious…"

"In you, Diana," Mika said, "you hold a special gift as well. One shared by our own species – a value and appreciation for truth as well as a dedication to the preservation of life. Each of you are the highlights of your species."

"Know this, each of you, that we may be far, but we will still be there, watching you, and in moments of greatest peril…"

"…protecting you," Mika added, looking down at Tristan, "just as you will be protecting her in your own special duty, Tristan."

"For she is special," Madonna added.

"Thank you," Tristan replied, nodding. "We won't let you down."

"Until our next encounter," Mika replied, bowing his head before stepping back. "Farewell."

The two of them stepped off and went to return to their shup Tristan stood with Diana as they watched. She then remembered.

"I almost forgot but remind me when we get home that I have a present for you," Diana said, tugging at Tristan's jumpsuit sleeve.

"What is it?" Tristan questioned, looking at her as he looked down at the ground himself.

"Actually, it'll be a surprise until your birthday," Diana replied, changing her mind. "It'll be a good time to reflect on all this."

"Jeez, why don't you just wait until Christmas?" Tristan sarcastically replied. "I can barely think forward to next week, and you're already thinking ahead to the next four months."

"Good idea," Diana replied with a smile. "Santa won't be bringing you any presents. You can wait until then."

Tristan laughed and grabbed Diana by her side.

"Alright then," Tristan smiled. "I think we should get going. I'm exhausted and just want to catch up one some sleep with my favorite gal. Let's go."

"Right answer," Diana replied, giving him a playful smile as they stepped off and joined the others while the sun shined and a peace settled in the air.

"Our servicemen and women are serving throughout the world as guardians of peace – many of them away from their homes, their friends, and their families. They are visible evidence of our determination to meet any threat to the peace with measured strength and high resolve. They are also evidence of a harsh, but inescapable truth – that the survival of freedom requires great cost and commitment, and great personal sacrifice."

– John F. Kennedy

www.ingramcontent.com/pod-product-compliance
Lightning Source LLC
Chambersburg PA
CBHW051432170626
46809CB00006B/2425